How many men these days, Dixie wondered, would go to such lengths to help a woman— to help her?

Dixie watched Erik silently for a moment, taking in a big whiff of the fresh mountain air and a large dose of the pleasant view of the ruggedly handsome man slapping his dust-lined black cowboy hat on his thigh and toeing the dirt with the tip of one scuffed boot.

Erik didn't say anything, but she knew what he must be thinking. How could she possibly follow through on this monumental project? She was obviously underqualified for this task in every way. Yet God had called her to the work here, made way the path of the Lord at every turn.

Last night, God had provided help in the form of a stray Border collie and a quiet cowboy who didn't appear all that enthused to have her hanging around in the first place.

Her angels.

She glanced again at Erik, wondering what he would think of being considered an angel in cowboy's clothing....

Books by Deb Kastner

Love Inspired

A Holiday Prayer #46
Daddy's Home #55
Black Hills Bride #90

DEB KASTNER

The wife of a Reformed Episcopal minister, it was natural for Deb to find her niche in the Christian/Inspirational romance market. She enjoys tackling the issues of faith and trust within the context of a romance. Her characters range from upbeat and humorous to—her favorite—dark and brooding heroes. Her plots fall anywhere between a playful romp and the deeply emotional.

When she's not writing, she enjoys spending time with her husband and three girls and, whenever she can manage, attending regional dinner theater and touring Broadway musicals.

Black Hills Bride
Deb Kastner

Love Inspired®

Published by Steeple Hill Books™

STEEPLE HILL BOOKS

ISBN 0-373-87096-5

BLACK HILLS BRIDE

Copyright © 2000 by Debra Kastner

This edition published by arrangement with Steeple Hill Books.

® and TM are trademarks of Steeple Hill Books, used under license.
Trademarks indicated with ® are registered in the United States Patent
and Trademark Office, the Canadian Trade Marks Office and in other
countries.

Visit us at www.steeplehill.com

Printed in U.S.A.

And behold, the Lord passed by, and a great and strong wind tore into the mountains and broke the rocks in pieces before the Lord, but the Lord was not in the wind; and after the wind an earthquake, but the Lord was not in the earthquake; and after the earthquake a fire, but the Lord was not in the fire; and after the fire a still small Voice.

—I Kings 19:11-12

To my mother, Ann Larkin,
for all your love and support.

And to the Last American Cowboy,
my grandfather, Gifford McIntosh.

Chapter One

If it wasn't heaven, it was certainly the next best thing. Dixie Sullivan's dreams were coming true in Technicolor, and she loved every moment. Sunshine, South Dakota and a horse of her own.

Okay, well, maybe not a horse. Not yet, anyway. But he was next on her list, and so far, her plans had gone without a hitch.

She pulled a deep, pine-laced breath of the crisp spring air of early April and surveyed the property. The land was certainly everything she expected it to be—covered with brush and lodgepole pines, scattered with a variety of woodland wildflowers.

Ever since her first vacation to South Dakota when she was thirteen, she knew she would someday return permanently and call South Dakota home.

Buying a spread of woodland in Custer was just her first step, and a baby step at that.

But nothing could daunt her today. She'd finally been able to step forward, putting the past behind her and looking head-on into her future. She'd even bought cowboy boots for the occasion, which, she thought, set off her indigo designer jeans nicely.

She might have made a mistake on the one-and-a-half-inch heels, which made it difficult to stay vertical at times on this rough terrain. But these boots had looked so much better than the flat-heeled ones. She didn't want to look like a cowpoke just because she was moving into the mountains.

She smiled. This was God's country, or at least it would be once she was done with it, she thought eagerly.

The buildings could be in better shape. She scratched a notation on a steno pad as she walked toward a dilapidated barn. The sawed pine was old and cracking, and there were many gaps in the walls.

Small house, large barn. And all of it falling apart. It looked very much like something built by a pioneer tending his first spread of land.

Dixie laughed. She was a pioneer in her own right, though she doubted the pioneer who settled this place had a wife with enameled, inch-long fingernails. She was a new breed, that was for sure.

She surveyed the notes she'd made and shook her head. A lot about this pioneer business was new to her. She'd have to learn by trial and error, she supposed. She hadn't asked how old the buildings were, and now she wished she had. She'd been so focused on finding the right amount of land for sale exactly where she'd hoped, the details were a bit of a blur.

You get what you pay for. And the land had come cheap. Miraculously so, especially when she offered to pay cash. God's blessing here left her more of the church's money for fixing the retreat up, making it look like the dream she and Abel Kincaid, her ex-fiancé, had carried in their hearts for so many years.

Or at least *she* had. Abel had his own agenda, one that ultimately didn't include her.

Thoughts of Abel weren't ever far from her mind, but she squared her shoulders and pushed them back. Now wasn't the time. And she wouldn't complain about the place needing a little elbow grease. Abel, a seasoned missionary, had prepared her for that contingency. She frowned and shoved the past to the back of her mind.

She had work to do.

It might take a bit more than elbow grease, though, she thought, running through figures in her head. Instead of renovating, she might have to start over and build from scratch.

It could be done, she decided, and probably should be.

Her guests would want modern facilities on the inside, however rustic-looking they might be on the outside. She doubted these buildings even had running water, a possibility confirmed by the presence of a pump outside the building designated as the main lodge.

Her eyebrows creased as she made another mark on her notepad. The main lodge would definitely have to be rebuilt. But what about the stable? She walked over to the oversize doors and pulled.

A loud *crack* was all the warning she got as the doors disintegrated into dust, raining a heap of splinters over her.

Shouting in surprise, she covered her head with her forearms, which took the brunt of the attack. Sharp-edged pieces split her skin wide, while large, blunt wood bruised her to the bone.

Shaken, she jumped back and put a palm to her chest to still her pumping heart. Her breathing came in short, audible gasps that scraped through her dry throat.

She groaned and tried to move her arms. She remembered being in a fistfight as a teenager, but that hadn't hurt this much. Several wounds were bleeding, but they weren't deep, Dixie decided, offering up a silent prayer of thanks, glad Someone was watching over her. Her expensive Western shirt was ruined, but she reminded herself it could have been worse.

Much worse.

She wrapped her sore arms around herself to keep

from shivering, though the day was warm. She could have been seriously injured, and she was alone on this ranch until she hired a foreman and a crew for the soon-to-be retreat lodge.

"Oh, Abel," she whispered, suddenly feeling very alone. And lonely. The past two years without Abel had been difficult. Not because she needed him—she'd never admit to that.

Hadn't she learned her lesson? She'd trusted Abel to be around when she needed him, and look where that got her. Certainly not South Dakota. She'd done that on her own.

She was a survivor, and Abel abandoning her wasn't enough to make her abandon the desire of her heart, the dream she nurtured and carried with her.

She turned her mind back to her work, not allowing herself to cling to her loneliness. The first thing she needed was a good foreman, someone to work by her side. A man, because despite her resolution to do it all on her own, she knew she had her limitations where physical strength was concerned, being only five foot one and a hundred pounds soaking wet.

She'd been asking around town, and the name Erik Wheeler cropped up more than once. She'd immediately started tracking him down to see if he was available for hire. At the moment he was her only real lead, and to say it was a warm lead would be exaggerating.

He hadn't returned her numerous phone calls, though she'd conscientiously kept her cell phone by her side. It frustrated her that she hadn't heard a word. The least he could do was call and say "No, thank you" if he wasn't interested.

A group from her home church in Denver were her first scheduled guests, but that was three months down the road, and three months was a long time for a woman on her own.

She'd have to be more careful moving around here until she knew just how safe—or *unsafe*—the place was. She surveyed her wounds, but didn't see anything that demanded her immediate attention. She'd wash up at the well—if it worked.

Sighing, she crouched down and poked a wary finger at what was left of the door, wondering if she could salvage any wood, even if it was just for kindling for a campfire.

She'd never made a campfire before, but it didn't look that difficult. She'd checked out scouting books from the library and had brushed up on the subject, along with a several hundred others she thought she might need in the wilderness.

As she stooped to pick through the wood, the hair suddenly pricked up on the back of her neck, and her breath clinched in her throat. She had the most disturbing notion that she wasn't alone, that someone's eyes were on her back.

She forced herself to breathe deeply a couple of times. Someone *was* watching her.

God.

And a whole legion of angels with Him, sent to protect her. She couldn't see them, but her faith confirmed they were present. The Bible said so, and that was enough for her.

God didn't take days off, she reminded herself with a shaky laugh. The broken door had startled her, that was all it was. A pretty reasonable reaction, all things considered.

But if she started letting her imagination run wild at this point, she was going to be in for a long, rocky ride. She might be alone for a couple more weeks yet, maybe longer, if the equivocal Mr. Wheeler stayed in hiding. There was nothing to be afraid of, as long as she was careful.

God was here.

With that reassuring thought firmly in place, she rose and dusted off her jeans, now more a dusty brown than indigo. She laughed quietly at herself.

She could really be a goose sometimes. Where was her faith?

She decided to check out the interior of the main house, reminding herself deprecatingly to keep an eye out for imploding doors. The thought made her laugh out loud at her own silliness. Whirling around to go the way she'd come, she plowed right into a man's rock-hard chest.

She would have fallen, but the man's arms snaked protectively around her waist, gripping her firmly but gently. She had an impression of breadth and build, but little else, with her nose buried as it was in his blue flannel shirt, which smelled of sweat and horse.

It was a very effective combination. Her heartbeat doubled.

She muttered a rather ineffective exclamation, being muffled by fabric as it was. She twisted uncomfortably in the man's grasp, unwilling to be held in so intimate a posture with a stranger.

His large, roughened hands were uncannily gentle, giving her another kind of fluttery, unsettled feeling in her chest, one she was less familiar with than the fear of injury or pain.

"Easy there," she thought she heard him whisper in a soothing baritone, but she decided she was mistaken when she looked up into his granite-featured face.

Piercing blue eyes, half-hidden by the brim of a black Stetson, met hers, and she nearly shivered at the lack of emotion in their depths. She'd seen stones with more life.

His thin, masculine lips were pressed together, giving Dixie the impression he was annoyed with something or someone. Probably her. She straightened her shoulders and composed her features as best she could.

"My name is Dixie Sullivan," she offered, dusting her palm against her pitifully dirty jeans before offering him her hand.

His glance dropped to her proffered hand, then rose back to her face. His expression didn't change. Neither did his posture.

After a moment, Dixie awkwardly withdrew her hand and stuffed it in her front pocket. The man made her nervous. Why didn't he speak? And it was downright rude to ignore a friendly handshake.

"I own this land?" she said as a question, leaving him to explain his presence here.

Still, he didn't move or speak. Dixie decided he was either a deaf-mute or the singularly most unfriendly, unpleasant man she'd ever met. He might be the best-looking cowboy she'd ever laid eyes on, but she fervently hoped he wasn't a close neighbor, someone she might be forced to interact with from time to time.

What an unpleasant thought! But why else would he be on her land?

He could be a poacher, but he didn't look like one, with scuffed black boots and a worn Stetson. He looked like a ranch hand.

Of course, she didn't *know* what a poacher looked like, but then, he wouldn't have walked up to introduce himself if he was hunting on her land, would he?

If introducing himself was, indeed, his intention.

If it was, he wasn't accomplishing his task with much success, she decided wryly. His continued silence put her on the defensive, making her more aware than ever that she was a woman on her own.

Abel wouldn't have had this problem. But then again, Abel wasn't a woman faced with a disturbingly attractive intruder.

She planted her hands on her hips and glared back at the cowboy. If he insisted on a staring match, he'd find her a worthy opponent. Though it would help if she could see his eyes better. He kept them well shaded under the brim of his hat, tucked away like whatever thoughts and feelings he possessed.

"And you are?" she asked pointedly, not really expecting an answer.

He surprised her. He stepped forward and pulled his hat off his head by the crown, exposing a thatch of thick black hair. "Erik Wheeler."

This was Erik Wheeler? The perfect-man-for-the-foreman-position Erik Wheeler? Dixie stared, astonished, into the most startling blue eyes she'd ever seen, made even more distinct by the deeply tanned face with the color and consistency of saddle leather.

She hadn't expected Erik Wheeler to be young. Or ruggedly handsome, not that she noticed. Didn't foremen have to be old men with paunches and a family of seven?

Clearly she had much to learn, and not from television, either. Her only experience with cowboys was old Westerns à la John Wayne, and she suspected that limited knowledge wouldn't help her now. Erik Wheeler definitely didn't look like the Western-movie type.

He was every inch the real thing, from the tips of his scuffed boots to the top of his alluringly tousled hair.

"I'm Dixie Sullivan," she said, then realized she'd already introduced herself. Heat flared to her face, making her even more annoyed. She wished she could keep what she was thinking from her expression, but she was dismally inept at keeping a straight face.

A smile flickered on his lips, then disappeared. "I know," he said, his voice low and soft.

"You've come about the foreman position?" It seemed the logical next question, but Dixie couldn't help but feel it was like pulling teeth to get Erik to answer. It wasn't exactly a personal question.

"Yep." He nodded and replaced his cowboy hat.

"I see." She paused while her thoughts raced. She should probably take him into her office and interview him properly.

Except she didn't have an office set up yet. What would Abel have done? She scowled. Never mind that—what was *she* going to do? Abel wasn't here, and she was.

She glanced at the main house, where she planned to build the big lodge, then back at Erik, who hadn't, in her observation, moved at all. He was shading his gaze with his hat again, she thought in annoyance.

She certainly wasn't prepared for his presence here. She planned to be neat and well-groomed, for starters, not in dusty, torn leftovers of designer Western clothes. She was certain her face must be equally smudged with dirt, and her usually immaculate, straight, shoulder-length black hair a tangled mess around her face.

Oh, what she wouldn't give for a long, hot, peach-scented bath right about now to wash away the grime and blood. The thought made her sigh inwardly.

Erik Wheeler hadn't returned a single phone call, yet here he was in person, obviously expecting something from her. Whatever *that* was.

She blew out a breath. "Okay. Well, you can see you caught me a little off guard."

"Yep," he agreed with a nod.

If he said *yep* one more time, she was going to scream.

This had been the longest day of her life. She was hot, tired and dirty. All she wanted right now was a warm bubble bath and a good book, but she wasn't even sure the main house, where she planned to stay—at least until it was torn down and replaced with a modern alternative—*had* a bathtub. She could only hope.

"Why don't you meet me over there, at the lodge," she said, gesturing. "I'll only be a minute. I'm going to run back to my truck and gather a few things I'll need for the interview."

"No interview," he said in a soft, rich baritone that belied his words and curled her toes.

No interview? If he wasn't here about the job, just exactly what *was* the rugged, handsome man doing on her property?

She was going to find out.

Chapter Two

❧

"Excuse me?" If she was put off by his cavalier attitude before, she was doubly so now.

"No interview," he said again.

"I'm sorry, Mr. Wheeler, but if you want this job, you're going to have to interview with me." She stood to her full height, but still only came to the middle of his chest.

He shrugged.

Taking that as a yes, she whirled around and hiked away from him, sending up a prayer for patience.

If Erik Wheeler was the best, she needed him. But she wasn't about to grovel and beg, no matter how desperate she was on the inside.

She was offering him a decent job, for goodness' sake. *With room and board.*

She cringed. He'd be much worse than a neighbor. If he took the position, she'd be rubbing elbows with him on a daily basis. She didn't know the first thing about running stables or leading trail rides, which meant she'd have to defer to his wisdom.

Mighty difficult if she couldn't get a word out of him, she thought crossly.

Loosen up, Dixie, she coaxed herself. Comfortable as she was to the hustle and bustle of the city, the relaxed pace of country living would take a little getting used to. Maybe everyone here contemplated their words before speaking, as Erik appeared to do.

Well, not everyone. The woman in the post office nearly prattled her ear off giving her all the latest town gossip a new resident was required to know.

Reaching her truck, she opened up the passenger door to the cab and dug through the papers stacked on the floor. Somewhere in this mess was a blank yellow legal pad and the three-ring binder with the notes she'd prepared to interview potential staff with.

It took her a full five minutes to locate the needed items. She half expected Erik to have vanished the way he'd appeared, but she found him waiting for her next to the main house, his arms crossed, lazily leaning his hip on what she assumed was an old hitching post.

All he needed was a long stem of hay between

his teeth and Dixie really would believe she'd been transported to another time and place.

She tried to quell the laughter bubbling in the back of her throat, but mirth squeaked out past her pressed lips despite her best efforts.

Erik pressed his own lips together to keep from joining in her laughter. It was an unusual reaction for him, to want to laugh, and it made him edgy. What was it about this tiny sprite of a woman that made him want to smile?

He tugged his hat lower on his forehead.

Crazy woman. Where did she get off thinking she could waltz onto a spread of land and magically transform it into a business? Or a ministry, or a retreat or whatever term she wanted to use.

For one thing, she was a woman on her own. And a beautiful woman at that, even if she did look like she'd been hog wrestling in the muck and lost. Dust couldn't hide the shine of her shoulder-length, satiny black hair, nor could smudges mar her peaches-and-cream complexion.

She didn't belong here. Her cowboy boots had heels on them, for crying out loud, and her clothes weren't something a person could pick up in a department store, he didn't think. And her fingernails—they'd last all of a day in these conditions.

He almost laughed, except that there was something distinctly not funny about the situation.

When he'd heard who bought the land, he'd done

a little digging to get the lowdown on Miss Dixie Sullivan, since her land rode with his meager spread. He'd found out all he needed to know, and her appearance here did nothing if not confirm his worst fears.

She was as green as a newborn filly where mountain living was concerned, and heading for disaster with every step she took. She ought to just take her pretty little freckles—all five of them scattered across her nose—not that he was counting—and skitter on back where she came from.

Cute as she looked in her new Western getup, she was a city girl from top to toe. She didn't belong here.

That's what he'd come to tell her, though she was obviously under the impression he was here for the foreman position.

He should have set her straight right away, he supposed, but talkin' to folks he didn't know, especially women, was equal to him with riding a bronc with a burr in its saddle.

She opened a squeaky screen door to the main house and gestured for him to come inside. Having subversively witnessed the barn door catastrophe, he chuckled when she eyed the doorframe as if it were going to reach out and grab her.

Her gaze was on him in a flash, suspicious and full of questions he really didn't want to answer.

"Mr. Wheeler?" she offered, gesturing for him to move inside.

"Erik," he corrected, tipping his hat off and reaching above her head to hold the door for her. The movement caused a whiff of her perfume to meander over him, and he inhaled deeply. Wasn't often he was this near a beautiful, fragrant woman.

Peaches and cream, he thought, like the lady herself. It took all his willpower not to lean in and inhale again. She stared up at him for a moment before letting out a breath and leading the way into the main house.

Her dismay at seeing the interior was evident on her face, giving him the oddest inclination to distract her from the mess. But what business was it of his? Surely she'd checked the place out before she bought it.

"I was told," she said, her voice cracking, "there was furniture in this old house. I thought it would at least be livable until..."

Oh, man, she was about to cry. "Please, God, don't let there be tears," he mumbled, though in truth he didn't believe God was listening.

He didn't believe there was a God at all, at least not the loving, merciful God his mother had spoken of—before that *merciful* God took her away, leaving his father to raise three small boys.

He tensed, shaken by the memory. He hadn't

thought of his mother for a long time, or what his father...

No. He wouldn't go there.

Turning his attention to Dixie, he mentally shook his head and crammed the lost-little-boy's feelings back into the recesses of his heart.

If there *was* a God, He sure wasn't helping this little lady, and she was professing to do His work.

He snorted his disdain, then pressed his lips together to keep from asking her why she didn't know the condition of the interior of this building. It was none of his business. It wasn't her fault his memories made him angry.

"Well," Dixie said, her expression gathering composure as she walked into the kitchen, "there's a table, at least. And a couple er—chairs."

Using the term loosely, he thought. *Logs* would be more accurate, but not wanting to point out the obvious, he pulled up a log and sat down, elbows on his knees. It made him feel as gangly as an adolescent. He frowned at the picture he must make, all elbows and knees.

She sat on a log facing him and put her notepad on the table. "I'm glad we don't have to eat this way," she said with a wavering smile, gesturing to the table, which came just below her chin. "I wasn't planning to use the furniture anyway, but I had hoped to live here until I can get some other things in order."

She looked at him as if she expected a response, and he grunted noncommittally. What did she expect him to say? That she was crazy even to consider it?

"Good thing I brought a tent along."

A *tent?*

He nearly stood up, so strong was his reaction. Now he *knew* the woman was certifiable.

She was planning to camp in a tent? He'd bet his last paycheck she didn't have a clue how to set it up, much less what kind of danger she was putting herself into. This wasn't Jellystone Park. And the bears here weren't after her picnic basket.

"Yep," he said at last.

And I'm a monkey's uncle, he added silently.

She glared at him, angry sparks shooting from her eyes. He curled the brim of his hat in his fist, wishing desperately it was polite to wear it in the house. His hat made him feel more comfortable; it was like a shield from the world.

Somehow he'd ticked her off. Seemed like everything he said was the wrong thing, though for the life of him, he couldn't figure out how *yep* could be construed as anything bad.

Oh, to be out with his horses, instead of squatting on a log with a beautiful woman. With his horses, he knew what to say, how to act. It was only around people he felt tongue-tied and awkward.

His horses.

He didn't have any horses. A spur dragged across

his gut, and he clenched his jaw. Now wasn't the time.

"Mr. Wheeler," Dixie said. "Erik," she amended when he narrowed his eyes on her. "I'm sure you've heard that I'm in the process of opening a retreat lodge here. Rockhaven Christian Center."

She smiled when she said the name. "It's going to be a place for church people to go when they need to get away from the hustle of the outside world and refocus their attention on God."

Did she really think she'd find God here? He barely restrained himself from shaking his head. Instead, he dropped his gaze to his hat so he wouldn't give his thoughts away.

"I want a big stable, with lots of horses."

The enthusiasm in her voice meandered into his chest, stirring the deepest desire of his heart. His gaze snapped to hers, and he swallowed hard. Her big, aqua-blue eyes swirled with the same intensity he felt.

Her words confirmed it. "I love horses, Mr.—uh, Erik. And I need a foreman to design and implement my program. Trail rides, hayrides, pony rides for the kiddies. Interested?"

Surprisingly he was. When he'd come here this morning, he had no intention of taking this job, but something about the way Dixie presented it made it sound appealing. And truth be told, he didn't have anything better to do.

"I expect we'll need to work closely to make sure everything goes without a hitch. No pun intended," she added, smiling.

She smiled with her shimmering eyes. A deep, inner glow that made him want to smile, too.

Yeah, he'd like to work with her, inhale more of her scent, ingest more of her laughter.

But he couldn't. Not even for her.

"I understand you're looking for your own herd, that you like to break horses in your spare time."

Her words penetrated into his thoughts, jolting him back to the present.

"Yep," he said. It concerned him that she knew so much about him. But Custer was a small mountain town, he reminded himself. No one kept a secret for long.

Suddenly the room felt cramped. He tugged at the collar of his flannel shirt. Though he wore the two top buttons open, he felt as if he were choking.

Dixie continued, ignoring his gesture. "I'm more than willing to accommodate your wishes. And there's plenty of land here. We can build you a corral just for your own work. As long as you keep it to your off-hours, you're free to break your own horses."

His breath stopped somewhere between his lungs and his throat and began to swell almost painfully. He did need a job, and what she was offering was more than he could have ever hoped for.

But how could *he* work for a Christian retreat? He wasn't a saint. Not anywhere close.

Dixie clasped her hands in her lap, wishing he'd look at her again. He seemed almost human when their gazes met, but then he'd look away and she'd lose the connection. He obviously felt he'd been given a small quota of words for a lifetime and was afraid he'd use them all up in his conversation with her, she thought, bristling.

"There's one more question," she said softly.

He met her gaze firmly and calmly.

"Are you a Christian, Erik?"

He immediately looked away. "No."

She nodded. "You are aware that this is a Christian retreat. Are you comfortable with that, and all it entails?"

He coughed, sounding as if he were choking, but a moment later his gaze met hers, and his eyes were clear. "Yep."

If she could get him beyond a *yep*.

Or at least get him to respond directly to her offer—then maybe *yep* wouldn't be *all* bad.

"I'll throw in a quarterly bonus. One horse. That's more than a fair deal, Mr.—uh, Erik."

She cringed inside, knowing it would take most of her own paycheck to make that bonus. Not so much for the money, but for the principle behind it.

It galled her that she needed a man to help her

make this work, but there it was. She needed Erik, even if it meant bribing him to take the job.

Abruptly he stood and slapped his hat against his knee, staring out the broken glass window next to the table.

She waited for him to speak, but of course he didn't.

After a silent moment, she stood and faced him off. "Will you come work for me?"

No more than a flicker of emotion passed through his dark blue eyes.

When she despaired of ever having an answer, his mouth tipped into what was almost a grin, and he slapped his hat on his knee again. "Yep."

Relief flooded her chest. The man didn't talk much, but from what she'd heard, he knew his way around a ranch. And she knew by their short conversation, however one-sided, that he shared her passion for horses. She'd seen that in his eyes.

In the back of her mind, she admitted to herself that there was a very personal reason she wanted Erik here. To teach her everything he knew.

To mold her love of horses into something concrete, something beyond mere fantasy. In her own spare time, she wanted to ride her very own horse through every inch of this land, to feel the power of thundering hooves beneath her and the wind whipping through her hair as she galloped across the meadow at top speed.

And Erik Wheeler could show her how.

She'd hoped to find a Christian foreman, but she supposed she couldn't be too picky, as far removed from a big city as she was. She only hoped she was distant enough from her emotions to choose the man for what he could do for the retreat, and not for what he could do for her personally.

But a decision had to be made, and made now, where Erik Wheeler was concerned.

She extended her hand to him, and this time he took it. He had a strong, firm shake, with broad, callused hands that had seen many years of hard labor. A country man, not afraid of a little hard work.

Work hard, play hard.

The quote came unbidden to her mind, and she smiled. She couldn't imagine this strong, silent cowboy *playing* at anything.

"If you could come back tomorrow, we can survey the damage to the barn and decide what needs to be built. I know this place doesn't seem like much, but it will be." Enthusiasm swelled in her heart as the finished picture entered her mind.

Happy children running around in front of the main lodge, bouncing toddlers taking pony rides, whole families spending quality time together with each other and the Lord.

"I'll need your help assessing the damage. And if I can get you to hire the work crews—I know we'll need carpenters and horsemen. You know the people in town better than I do.''

She added silently that if everyone in Custer was as hard a sell as Erik Wheeler, she was never going to get her retreat finished in time for her church family to make their visit.

Absently she reached out for her notepad. She barely leaned on the table, but that was all it took.

The table cracked loudly, and she jumped back, startled. Her notepad went airborne, papers flying every which direction. And the heap of wood that had once been the table looked no more salvageable than the stable doors had been. Firewood at best; and at worst, another mess for her to clean up.

''Not again!'' she wailed, then clamped her mouth shut when she realized Erik was listening. She didn't want to appear to be losing faith in front of him.

But it had been a very long day.

''Lady,'' he drawled slowly, then paused.

She whirled at the sound of his chuckle.

The corner of his mouth tipped into a crooked grin. ''You've got a lot of work to do.''

Chapter Three

Erik chuckled all the way back to the dump of a mobile home planted on his pathetic little piece of land. He scanned the familiar rolling hills and sighed.

Not even enough room for a small herd of horses, never mind what he envisioned if things were the way he wanted them to be.

But then things never were. He'd learned that as a child. Best he keep his thoughts to himself and just do whatever the little lady and her grand ideas dictated.

She'd learn the hard truth soon enough. And that'd put him out of a job again. But maybe, if she lasted long enough, he might be able to manage to get a green broke colt and filly out of it.

A good solid quarter horse stallion and a feisty

Arab mare. The best of both worlds. If he were allowed to pick his own stock, that is.

It would be the break he needed, the opportunity he'd been waiting for. Adrenaline rushed through him just thinking about it. His own herd of horses. Eventually he could get a better tract of land, and then—

He cut his own thoughts short. He knew he was dreaming. But there was a very real possibility he could humor her along for that one chance to get back on his feet again and make something of himself. It was a small price to pay, all things considered.

His biggest problem was the woman herself. Dixie Sullivan was one stubborn woman. He'd realized that from the time the stable door fell crashing down on top of her. That alone would have stopped most people right in their tracks.

And she'd just dusted off her fancy designer jeans and plowed on.

In the general way of things, he made it a practice to keep his nose out of other people's business. All a man got from meddling was a sore nose.

The corner of his mouth made the tiniest quirk as he appreciated his own humor.

But that still left him with a beautiful, helpless city woman determined to camp out alone on her land with nothing more than a tent.

She knew nothing about these woods, nothing

about camping out, yet she was determined to break this bronc single-handedly. Stubborn woman.

And tongue-tyingly beautiful.

Erik's black-and-white Border collie, Lucy, trotted up to him from where she'd been lying in the shade of a pine. She barked hello and he leaned down to rub behind her ears, making a low, pleasant growling sound from the back of his throat that elicited the same response in her.

She barked again and made a play-bow, her tail wagging in anticipation. He smiled down at her, glad for her companionship, the only one who liked having him around.

He'd rescued her as a pup, when, as the runt of the litter and having one blue eye and one brown eye, she was going to be drowned. Poor little thing. His heart had got the best of him, and he'd taken her home. Lucy suited him just fine, and he suited her.

Lucy was the one female he trusted, a little reminder of stability in a world gone haywire. She always acted in a predictable way, and she never expected him to talk. Quiet, peaceful companionship with few expectations.

If only human females shared the same traits.

Lucy brought him a stick and he threw it for her, his mind wandering back to his predicament. If Dixie listened to his advice, she wouldn't be putting herself in any danger, which is exactly what she was doing with that ridiculous tent notion of hers.

The commonsense thing for her to do would be to check into a motel in Custer until the work on the place was finished, if it ever got that far. But when he'd suggested as much, she just shook her head and fervently declined. She didn't, she informed him in an icy tone, need anyone to watch over her. She was fine on her own, thank you very much.

Except for the bears, wolves and who knew what other scavengers might just be waiting to prey on her, he'd reminded her. And she hadn't even batted an eyelash at his poorly concealed threat.

Okay, maybe he was exaggerating a little about the animals, but it had been known to happen. Rare, but possible. Especially since the land she was on hadn't been used much recently.

It was none of his business what that crazy woman did or didn't do. If a bear ate her, it would serve her right.

Lucy dropped the stick in his palm and he tossed it for her again.

He should forget about her, he decided with a frown. Her problems didn't concern him. But even as he thought it, he whistled for Lucy to come back to him.

"C'mon, girl," he growled reluctantly. "Let's go see how the little lady's managing."

The *little lady* wasn't *managing* at all. In fact, she was lying faceup on a flat bed of canvas, staring at the bright-blue Dakota sky and wondering if pioneers really did sleep under the stars.

Because that's what she was going to be doing if she didn't get her act together and this stupid tent off the ground. And at this point it looked pretty hopeless.

The box said Easy Assembly in big letters. Ten Minutes, it said. No Tools Needed.

Ha! She expected she needed at *least* a hammer and a hundred nails to get the tent to stand. A hammer she had, but other than the pegs that came in the box, she was out of business.

In theory it was simple. She pushed the long, plastic tubes through all the little canvas tunnels, and then the bundle of rumpled material was supposed to transform into something she could sleep in.

Not *on. In.*

But every time she tried to stand it up, it made a funny springing sound and fell into a heap. She stared at the lines and pegs, with which she was supposed to tie off the tent when it was assembled.

Assembled, hah!

Maybe she should go back to town and stay in a motel room, as Erik had suggested. At least for the night. It had been a hard day, after all, and nothing sounded more appealing than a long, hot bubble bath. The idea was tempting.

But it wouldn't happen. She would not, could not, give up on this tent. In a way, it represented her whole endeavor. If she quit every time something went wrong, she knew she'd be packing for Denver by the end of the month.

And she couldn't let that happen. She hadn't even purchased her horse yet.

Besides, it wouldn't do to let Erik know he was right. The man was cocky enough as it was, telling her what to do, as if she couldn't make up her own mind.

The thought spurred her into action. Throwing some choice nicknames at the inanimate bundle of chaos, she stood up and walked around the perimeter of the tent, narrowing her eyes at the wretched canvas and frowning in concentration.

"Father, I'm in trouble again." She didn't worry about praying aloud. There wasn't a soul within miles of here. "I've got to get this tent up, but I've failed several times. Help me, God. Give me wisdom. And if You've got a minute, a little heavenly intervention would be greatly appreciated."

Always start with prayer, her mother used to say.

Her heart stung as if popped with the end of a bullwhip. In her exuberance to be truly out on her own, she'd forgotten the importance of prayer before action, and look where it had got her.

She sure hoped God was a better camper than she was.

She glanced at the pegs again and got an idea. If she tied the tent up one pole at a time and pegged it out, it would have to stay up, eventually. And then she could fix the wobbles.

She smiled and reached for her hammer. If God blessed her pathetic efforts, she might not need those hundred nails after all.

She laughed out loud, and the sound echoed through the small valley. She thought she heard a dog barking in response, coming from the edge of the small meadow. She peered in that direction, but the trees hid everything from view.

Oh well, a stray dog or two in the area wasn't a problem. She liked dogs.

Carefully she tied off the first pole, then pulled it taut and hammered the peg into the grass.

"There," she said aloud, wiping her hands together and smiling with satisfaction. "I knew I could do it."

Her triumph was short-lived, however, as the tent began to waver toward her.

"Oh, no. Oh, no. Don't you do this to me," she said, not realizing she was yelling.

Moments later she was covered by canvas.

As she wriggled under the weight of the collapsed tent, she heard the dog bark again and hoped he was alone. It was humiliating enough to have this happen to her without anyone seeing her.

This was private property, but Erik Wheeler certainly hadn't been bashful about coming onto her land without announcing himself. For all she knew, invading a person's privacy and property was a normal part of small-town mountain living.

She crawled out from beneath the canvas, spitting out the pieces of grass caught between her teeth.

Yuck! And there was dirt under her inch-long nails. Good thing they were made of enamel, or they'd all have broken off by now.

When she heard another bark, she surveyed the edge of the woods quite thoroughly, even going through a few of the trees and calling for the pup, but she didn't see any sign of dog or man.

Maybe her overworked mind was concocting a dog from nowhere. Hadn't she lain awake in bed for nights before moving here, considering the worst the land could offer?

Bears, wolves, mountain lions and who knew what else.

God knew.

The thought reassured her. She shook her head, dusted off her jeans and went back to work, pole by pole. And this time, glory be, it worked.

She anchored the two opposite sides, then finished off the rest of the poles and pegs, too tired to even appreciate her success.

In the end, it was a little wobbly, but it would do, at least for tonight.

She'd never been so tired in her life. Every single muscle in her body ached, including some she hadn't even known existed until today. It hurt even to breathe.

It took all the force of her will to compel her exhausted, aching body to move. She went back to the truck and unloaded three large cardboard boxes full of food and a cooler of cold soda—her groceries for the month—and placed them next to the front door of her tent.

She meant to put them in the two-room tent with her, but she was too weary to even consider it. They'd be okay where they were for the night.

She wandered around looking for firewood for about ten minutes before yawns overtook her, and she decided she was too tired to eat, never mind to start a fire. She doubted if her brain could even recall how to make one, if she had enough wood, which she doubted.

Oh, well. Hopefully it wouldn't get too cold tonight. It was still early spring.

She hoped it wouldn't snow, although, with the way things had been going since she got here, she wouldn't be surprised if it snowed five feet.

Dragging her Eskimo-hood sleeping bag into the tent, she crawled into her warm cocoon and immediately felt drowsiness overtake her, clouding her mind and easing the ache in her limbs.

Every other catastrophe would just have to wait until she had a good night's sleep.

Chapter Four

Erik trod carefully from Dixie's campsite, but inside he was running. Running for his life.

Fool woman. She'd grabbed her sleeping bag and headed for the tent without so much as taking care of her supplies! Didn't she have even the vaguest knowledge of what it meant to live in the mountains? This wasn't a secure penthouse apartment with a hulking doorman security guard to protect her—not to mention her food, gear and supplies.

Not my problem.

He repeated it over and over in his mind, but his heart didn't agree. He scowled, annoyed with himself. But mostly, annoyed with her.

He shouldn't have been spying on her in the first place, he chided himself. He'd intruded on an intensely personal moment, one she'd be mortified over if she ever discovered someone had witnessed it.

Heat crept up on his face, making his scowl deepen. He was no gawking teenager or Peeping Tom, even if the woman in question made his gut do a funny little dance when he looked at her.

He should know better.

She was going to have to learn the hard truth of how unprepared she really was, one way or another. Maybe a night alone in the woods was just what she needed to make her tuck her tail and run for the city.

That's what he wanted, wasn't it?

Yeah, he supposed he did, but not quite so soon. Not until he had two horses, at least. Which meant she had to last a half a year.

No. It meant a whole lot more than that. It meant he'd have to keep her *out of trouble* for a half a year. Crazy, stubborn woman!

He paused and looked back.

Lucy sat down at his feet and whined.

He grunted in response. Even his dog was nagging at him to go back.

"Think so, do you?" He lifted his hat from his head and wiped his brow with his sleeve, though the spring evening was crisp. "You would stick up for another female."

Lucy whined again and barked, two short yips and a long, well-enunciated growl.

"Yeah, maybe so," he agreed, sauntering around

to look in the direction from which he came. He leaned his shoulder against a lodgepole pine and hooked his thumb through a belt loop.

He could go back on her land and hide in the trees, taking the midnight watch, so to speak. But that would be trespassing.

No, worse. It would be spying. Again. He shook his head, determination to save his own skin winning out over an absurd sense of chivalry. He was nobody's cowboy but his own.

"Nah."

At the single word, Lucy growled low and barked once. He could swear she was scowling at him.

"Mother hen," he complained with a chuckle. "I don't care if you disagree."

He crouched down to wrap an arm around the dog, scratching her ears with his thumb.

She wriggled out of his grasp and sat down a foot away from him, staring at him through her mismatched eyes.

"I know, I know. You think I'm a big oaf. And maybe I am. But I can't spy on her, even if it's for her own good. You don't understand what a good-lookin' woman like her does to a man's soul."

Lucy cocked her head and whined.

"End of subject!" he said more firmly than he intended.

Lucy trotted a few steps back the way they'd

come, then turned to look back at him. When he didn't move, she barked sharply.

"I'm not coming," he said firmly. "I don't know when you thought you earned the title of Leader of the Pack, but I'm not budging. Not a chance."

To confirm his point, he crossed his arms over his chest with a quiet huff.

He could have sworn she shrugged as she turned her back on him and padded off down the road toward Dixie. She stopped again just before a bend in the path that would take her out of his sight and implored him with her large collie eyes.

"No," he said again, hardly believing he was arguing with his dog, yet finding an odd sort of humor in it. Dixie had only been here for less than a day, and she already changed his life in more ways than one.

Like turning his own dog against him, for one thing. Suddenly an idea hit him.

"Well, yeah, of course! I see what you mean." He chuckled aloud.

He might be an unwelcome lurker in Dixie's part of the woods, but she could hardly blame him for having Lucy there. Even if she did see the dog, she'd never know who her owner was.

And he felt at least as safe with Lucy guarding over Dixie as he would were he to spend the night outside her tent himself. She was well trained—better trained than he was for watchdog duty, he thought, smiling for the second time today.

Lucy could handle whatever came around—he'd bet his paycheck on it. He was off the hook, and Dixie would be safe.

More to the point, *he'd* be safe. No explanations necessary.

"Go on, girl," he told his dog, giving her his blessing. "You keep an eye on our Dixie, girl. She'll be safe and sound with you watching her."

Lucy barked and leapt out of sight.

He knew without a doubt she'd do exactly what needed to be done. Dogs had a sense about them for people in need, and Dixie Sullivan fit into that category whether she knew it or not.

As the strain and tension drained from his shoulders, he sighed and turned, beginning the long walk back to his suddenly achingly empty house.

Chapter Five

Dixie awoke with a start. She was certain she'd heard the low, deep growl of some ferocious animal, but as she strained to listen, the sound didn't repeat itself. She put a hand to her heart to settle its erratic thumping and rolled back into her bag.

She must have been dreaming. The exhaustion of a hard day was just catching up with her. It wasn't like a bear was going to come calling.

And then she heard it. To the casual ear, it sounded like scratching, with an occasional paper bag ripping open. But to Dixie, it meant someone—or something—was in the only food supply she had for three weeks, until her next check from the church arrived.

Anger hit her first, coursing through her. She jumped up so fast, she became tangled in her sleeping bag and fell in a painful and undignified heap. Unfortunately for her, aching muscles hadn't magically disappeared while she slept, however much she'd prayed they would.

With a muffled groan, she rolled over and tried again, this time managing to free her feet from the confining folds of the bag before trying to stand.

Once she was standing and stable, she stomped noisily toward the door of the tent, with every intention of going out to tell the overly ambitious animal to take a hike.

She kneeled down and reached for the zipper, then froze midreach, panic surging through her.

Exactly *what* kind of animal was rummaging through her supplies?

A bear.

A *bear!* What was she supposed to do when confronted with a bear? Stare them in the eye. No.

Don't make eye contact. Look at the floor. Try to look unappetizing. Turn and run.

No.

Freeze. And then what? Offer herself as dessert?

She frowned and forced air into her lungs. She was being a little farfetched.

It couldn't be a bear.

Okay, it could be. But it wasn't likely. So what, then? Wolves were common, and foxes, and mountain lions. What else? Nothing she wanted to deal with, especially on her own.

And she was definitely on her own. Fear and frustration quickly replaced anger.

What on earth was she supposed to do? Since she was already on her knees, she clenched her hands together in her lap and prayed.

Then she heard a low growl, and a new wave of apprehension washed through her.

Relax. But she couldn't.

Think. Not much better.

Concentrate!

If her ears weren't letting her down, the growl in question was distinctly canine. Her throat tightened, forcing the breath from her lungs.

The thought of tangling with a snarling wolf was only marginally better than the thought of tangling with a bear. She shivered, though the night was warm.

What if more than one kind of animal was out there?

She wrung her hands in her lap. *What to do?*

She heard her grocery bags rustling until another growl came from the other end of the tent. Her mind raced through her extremely limited and definitely secondhand knowledge of wild animals.

Wolves.

Wolves moved in packs, so likely it was wolves, if they were on both sides of her tent. Had they surrounded her?

How would she escape?

Think.

It might be foxes, but she couldn't recall if foxes growled, never mind if they moved in packs.

Wolves. *Wolves!*

What did one do to fend off wolves? Frustration and fear battled for prominence, twisting her stomach into hard knots.

Fire.

She'd seen that in a movie once.

Peachy. She recalled too late she'd been too tired to light a campfire. She had matches in the tent, but nothing to use as a torch came to mind.

There were things outside she could use, but that meant facing whatever was out there.

Could she do it?

Alone. So dreadfully, fearfully alone.

Dear Lord. It was all the prayer she could manage through her blurred and frantic mind.

Taking a shaky breath, she decided to attempt to sneak out of the tent without being seen. It was her only chance. She couldn't just sit in here and do nothing, waiting for them to do whatever it was wolves did with frightened humans.

She had some old rags and a bottle of lighter fluid with the supplies. If she could find a decent branch, she might be able to put together a torch and scare away the wolves.

Or else she'd be dessert, since they were obviously having dinner on her account right now, if the sound of shredding boxes and the crackling of wrappers was anything to go by.

Slowly, quietly, she unzipped the tent.

It stuck, and her heart lurched into her throat.

She closed her eyes and prayed fervently. The growling became louder and more distinct, and her breath caught as she wondered if she'd already been discovered.

"In for a penny," she quoted through gritted teeth, then yanked on the zipper. It moved, sliding the rest of the way up the doorway.

Thank God.

She remained still for a moment as her eyes adjusted to the darkness, and then began crawling slowly toward her supplies.

She didn't see any movement, and the air was crisp and abnormally silent. No cricket chirping laced the air. No owls hooting. Not even the scratching of paws on her boxes.

Silence. She wanted to scream to ease the tension. She bit her lip, hard.

At least, for the moment, she didn't see any big, furry objects. She could be thankful for that, anyway.

No wolves.

Maybe the animal or animals had left. She inched toward her supplies, wincing as loose gravel cut into her knees and palms.

Four feet to go, then two.

The closer she moved to her supplies, the louder her heart pounded in her ears, to the point where she wondered if she would be able to hear anything else.

Paradoxically her senses were overdefined from adrenaline, crystal clear and amplified. Strained to tautness, she thought she might break. Despite the fact that she could see and hear nothing out of the ordinary, she couldn't shake the eerie feeling she was being watched.

When she was within an arm's length of the nearest box, she took a deep breath and held it, then slid forward, reaching for the box behind it, the one containing the rags and lighter fluid.

Her hand was poised just above the boxes when a whiz of fur popped up from behind the box. Startled beyond belief, she fell backward onto the gravel, exclaiming in pain as the small, sharp rocks bit into her palms.

Two dark, beady eyes were staring back at her from behind a black mask, and the intruder told her off with a full minute of chattering.

A true bandit.

He was the biggest, meanest-looking raccoon Dixie had ever laid eyes on, not that she'd seen many. For some reason, she'd always assumed raccoons were gentle creatures—and considerably smaller than the one staring her down.

The menacing raccoon appeared to be angry with

her for interrupting his dinner, chattering angrily and waving his paws.

She stiffened, affronted by the raccoon's rude behavior. It was *her* food, after all, and he was the uninvited guest.

Would *"Shoo"* work with an animal his size?

She was on the verge of standing when the raccoon leaned forward, still chattering incessantly.

Was he poising for attack?

Her mind flew as she considered what to do. She'd never heard of a raccoon attacking a person before, but that didn't mean it hadn't happened. Especially out here in the wilderness.

Think!

This particular raccoon was clearly aggressive and not the least bit afraid. He hadn't run when she approached. And hadn't she read somewhere raccoons carry rabies?

Was this raccoon rabid?

She squinted, trying to see his mouth in the dark. She thought rabid animals foamed at the mouth. She didn't think this fellow was foaming.

All of the sudden, the raccoon hissed and ran toward her. She backed away crab-style, kicking gravel at the terrifying animal.

In the same moment, she felt something fast and furry brush past her left shoulder. Instinctively she ducked and tucked her head to her knees, preparing to be eaten alive.

When nothing happened, she dared a quick peek through her fingers. She heard a growl, and half expected to be a midnight snack for both raccoon and wolf.

She didn't know which was worse.

Instead, she found herself looking at the shaggy, unkempt fur of a black-and-white Border collie who'd planted herself between Dixie and the violent raccoon, teeth bared.

What Dixie couldn't do took the dog only seconds, as she chased the raccoon away from the supplies and off into the night. Dixie leaned back on her heels and concentrated on steadying her breathing.

Whether or not the dog was wild, she came back to where Dixie crouched, nestling her head against Dixie's chest with a soothing whine. She had one blue eye and one brown, but Dixie didn't care, for they were friendly, gentle eyes, and she needed a friend right now.

She buried her head in the dog's fur, thanking God and the dog for interceding.

She wondered why the dog hadn't chased away the raccoon before Dixie had left the tent. It was almost as if she was there to protect Dixie herself. However it had happened, she knew God had sent this dog here with a purpose; it was an angel in disguise.

The collie had literally saved her life, she realized as fear turned to tears.

She sniffled against the dog, which whined again and moved deeper into Dixie's arms, consoling her with the warmth of her fur.

As Dixie's heartbeat slowed and relief released the tension in her muscles, weariness overtook her. Still ultra aware of possible lurking animals, she checked over her supplies, trying, hoping and praying to find something salvageable.

But it was gone. All of it.

There went the dream of buying her own horse, floating up and away from her like smoke. She'd have to use her savings to feed herself.

It was too much to bear thinking about, so she stacked up the torn boxes in a haphazard pile and decided to go back to bed. Nothing more could be done in the dark of night. She'd have to get groceries in the morning.

She considered starting a fire, but decided against it. She wasn't positive she could have used a torch to fend off an attacking animal, in any case.

The lure of her toasty-warm sleeping bag called to her, reminding her how little sleep she'd had in the past week, what with her anticipation of moving and the millions of little details she'd had to attend to.

She let out a long sigh that turned into a yawn, and shuffled wearily back to her tent.

"Here, puppy," she called when she got to the edge of the tent, but the Border collie hung back.

She sighed again and shook her head, feeling vaguely disappointed the dog wouldn't follow her into the tent. She had the silly notion to keep the dog. She wasn't wearing any tags, and it only seemed right to reward the scruffy pup for saving her life.

The collie obviously had other plans. Besides, she was obviously tame and used to people. She probably belonged to someone around here. One of her neighbors, perhaps. A rancher, most likely.

She rolled back into her sleeping bag, ignoring the impulse to pull it over her head and hide. When the Border collie left, she'd be alone. Again.

Nothing new there.

Why should she be surprised? And why should it still hurt so much?

Her whole life had been one abandonment after another. First her mother, abandoning Dixie to her father so she could "live her own life," unburdened by an infant daughter.

Then Abel, deciding Pakistan was more important than marrying her. The ring on her finger had meant nothing—less than nothing.

She'd think she'd be used to it by now, but the sting of rejection still haunted her, even when she was rejected by nothing more than a stray dog she'd never seen before in her life.

To her surprise and delight, she saw a brief movement at the front of the tent and heard a low, now-familiar growl. The dog settled down just outside the front door, continuing to act as her guardian.

It was more than enough security for Dixie, wild animals or no wild animals. She had a guardian angel watching over her.

With the Border collie as her sentry, it wasn't as difficult as she'd imagined to fall into a deep, if troubled, sleep.

Chapter Six

Dixie was coming at him like a red-eyed bull, leaving a trail of dust behind her. Erik folded his arms over his chest and dug his booted heels in, refusing to give in to the impulse flooding over him to bolt like a young calf.

She'd told him to meet her in front of the future lodge at 8:00 a.m. sharp.

And here he was. A man of his word.

He bit on the corner of his lip and frowned. It was bad enough to have the woman coming at him with a bee in her bonnet, but it was infinitely worse to know he put it there himself.

He knew better.

He *knew* better than to stick his nose where it didn't belong. He *knew* better than to offer his hand to help another human being. He *knew* better than to care.

But when Lucy dragged him from bed at four o'clock in the morning, barking her head off and licking his rough, unshaved cheek, his first thoughts were of Dixie.

Had she lasted the night in her pitifully set-up tent? Had she had any more mishaps since he'd left her the night before?

He'd been relieved to find her tent still intact, though it looked as if she'd had her fair share of problems. Her food supply was trashed. Completely gone. It looked like a pack of wild animals had had themselves a real party.

For some annoying reason, he felt responsible for the pretty young lady who courageously bit off so much more than she could ever hope to chew. He knew it would get him into trouble. But he couldn't help it. He cared about the woman about to run him down.

Dixie steamed to a halt directly in front of him and tilted her head up to pierce him with her sharp, sparkling aqua gaze. He swept his hat from his head out of habit, in deference to a lady.

From the looks of things, a lady about to detonate like a time bomb.

Trying to appear casual and unconcerned, he leaned a hip on the hitching post. He attempted to divert his thoughts from the upcoming confrontation, turning his attention to the monumental task ahead of him, and marveling at the strength of the old wood against which he rested.

The place was falling down around him, but the hitching post didn't budge under the force of his weight, proving itself every bit as solid as the lump in his throat.

"Mr. Wheeler."

"Erik," he protested gruffly.

He watched her expression mold as she gathered her emotions and prepared himself for the worst. Of course she'd be angry. He was meddling.

He'd be mad, if he were in her place, far too proud to accept charity, however well meant, and however offhand that gift had been.

She might be as dangerous as a bull in a china shop with her sculptured nails and designer jeans, but Dixie Sullivan was a proud, stubborn woman.

And sure as shooting, he'd offended her.

He didn't know whether to be amused or petrified when she set her jaw. Avoiding her eyes, his gaze drifted to the pulse pounding against the soft skin at the base of her neck.

He swallowed hard, but the lump refused to dislodge.

Here it comes.

"I..." she began, then paused, her eyebrows creasing into a frown as she broke eye contact and looked at her brand-spanking-new cowboy boots.

Her fists clenched and unclenched. She looked as if she were fighting a war within herself.

Probably didn't know which kind of idiot to call him first.

"Thank you," she said at last, in a whisper he could barely hear.

The air rushed from his lungs as if she'd punched him.

Thank you?

He frowned and shook his head.

"I know it was you," she accused in a whisper, her sparkling eyes daring him to deny it, her full red lips pursing.

He couldn't deny anything, of course. He was the guilty party. But he shook his head again, just the same. Principle of the matter.

"I really—" Her voice cracked, and for a fraction of a second, he saw through the tough veneer to the sweet, vulnerable woman inside.

His mental reaction was sharp and immediate. The same frantic blaring in his head as when he found a baby calf caught in barbed wire, only worse.

Much worse.

Fortunately for him, her vulnerable look was immediately replaced with resentment. Or maybe not so good, he thought as she fisted her hands on her hips.

"I'm grateful," she ground out, sounding as if she were anything but. "However, I want to make it very clear that I do *not* want you thinking that just because you're my foreman, you have any obligation to take care of me.''

He held up his hands palms out. Where did that sudden outburst come from? He lifted a brow, asking without asking.

"I'm perfectly capable of taking care of myself.''

He shrugged. He wasn't going to argue with her.

Her cheeks turned the color of ripe peaches. ''I mean, I know it looks like I messed up last night.''

He raised both brows.

"Okay, I *did* mess up," she admitted, her voice coarse. ''But I don't need a man to tell me what to do.''

Ah, there was the burr in her saddle. She'd been jilted. Erik didn't like the way his stomach clenched as tight as his fists as he thought of the man who'd broken Dixie's heart.

"Who was he?''

Her eyes snapped to his, surprise and pain swirling through their aqua depths. ''I beg your pardon?''

He swallowed hard. ''The guy who made you so mad.''

She scowled, and he half expected her to yell at him that it was none of his business.

Instead, she blew out a breath and shook her head. ''It wasn't like that.''

Erik shrugged.

"No, really. I was—'' She paused and wet her

lips with the tip of her tongue. "I was engaged to a missionary. We would've been here together getting this retreat off the ground."

He grunted noncommittally, but inside he was straining to hear more of what made Dixie the woman who stood before him now.

"His name was Abel Kincaid. He decided to go back to South Asia instead of marrying me."

He expected anger and pain in her voice, but instead heard respect and longing.

"He was following God's call," she finished, her voice firm with conviction.

Kincaid must have been out of his mind to leave such a sweet, kindhearted woman behind, even to follow God. *Especially* to follow God.

"Why'd you do it?" she asked abruptly, her voice ending on a quiver.

His breath froze in his lungs, and though he opened his mouth to speak, no sound emerged. How could he tell her why he'd raced off to town this morning, calling in a favor to the local grocer, replacing her food as best he could in strong plastic containers, protected as it should have been in the first place?

How could he tell her what he didn't know himself?

Dixie read the odd combination of anxiety and compassion in his eyes and decided it more than made up for his lack of words. Who would have known underneath that rough, tough cowboy exterior was a kind, caring man with a heart of gold?

It reassured her about her choice of a foreman, removing the doubts that had plagued her since she'd woken this morning.

Somehow he'd found out about the raccoon incident before she'd even risen for the day. She never slept late, but today it had been after nine when she'd finally woken.

Only to find out he'd discovered her weakness. He'd found proof positive she was every bit the novice he'd accused her of being.

She'd even broken one of her nails, she realized belatedly, wondering why she wasn't as miffed about the discovery as she should be—or at least as she would have been a few days ago, before her foray into the South Dakota wilderness.

She was learning the tough realities of her new world, and it appeared she was learning most everything the hard way.

Things that appeared important in her sheltered middle-class suburban experience—her manicured fingernails, flawless complexion and perfect makeup—were considerably less of an issue in the rough terrain of mountain living.

No one here cared what brand of jeans a woman wore, or where she'd had her hair done. It was different here. Strange, sometimes frighteningly so.

She'd adjust. She had to. But she owed Erik a tremendous debt.

The truth was, had he not replaced her food supply, she would have had to give up her dream of owning her own horse. The church money was already allocated. She couldn't spend a penny of it, not even to feed herself in a crisis.

Her own money, her pitiful excuse for a life savings, was allocated, as well—to buying a horse of her own. But if push came to shove, she would have had to use that money on food.

But, of course, he didn't know that. He didn't know anything about her. He just happened to be chivalrous, though she couldn't imagine for the life of her why he'd done something so kind and wonderful for *her*.

How many men these days, she wondered, would go to such lengths to help a woman—help *her*?

And Erik had not only rescued her, he'd rescued her dreams. Her heart swelled with emotion and gratitude for the rough cowboy who'd entered her life with the quiet force of the center of a tornado.

She could do without a roof over her head, wild animals notwithstanding. But eating was pretty much of a necessity. She grinned wryly at her own humor, however depressing the situation was in reality.

And the funniest part—or maybe it wasn't funny

at all—was the gift she'd found between the plastic boxes. A pair of cowboy boots.

A *real* pair of cowboy boots—the short-heeled variety. She didn't know whether to be pleased or angry.

Either way, she couldn't stay beholden to this man, even if it meant she did, in fact, have to give up her own dreams for a while. She'd waited this long, hadn't she?

"Please allow me to repay your kindness," she pressed. "How much do I owe you?"

Erik made a sound that sounded suspiciously like choking, and Dixie wondered if he was offended. Or was he laughing at her?

She couldn't tell. She knew if she looked into his eyes, she'd know for certain—but he vigilantly looked everywhere but at her.

She watched him silently for a moment, taking in a big whiff of the fresh mountain air and a large dose of the pleasant view of the ruggedly handsome man slapping his dust-lined black cowboy hat on his thigh and toeing the dirt with the tip of one scuffed boot.

"Shall we get started with today's workload?" she asked at last, realizing he wasn't going to broach the subject of money no matter how hard she pushed him. And she certainly couldn't stare at him all day, as nice as the sight was.

He nodded, looking distinctly relieved.

She faltered over a laugh, assaulted by a sudden attack of nerves. Erik didn't say anything, but she knew what he must be thinking.

How could she possibly follow through on this monumental project?

She was obviously underqualified for this task in every way. Undersized, understaffed and underqualified.

Hadn't last night proved as much?

Yet God had called her to the work here, made way the path of the Lord at every turn.

Even last night, when she'd felt more alone than she had since Abel announced he was going back to South Asia, God had provided help in the form of a stray Border collie and a quiet cowboy who didn't appear all that enthused to have her hanging around in the first place.

Her angels.

She glanced again at Erik, wondering what he would think of being considered an angel in cowboy's clothing. A smile twitched at the corner of her mouth.

She thought he might object.

"Actually I have very little idea on where to start," she admitted candidly, looking around and sighing loudly. "Nothing in my education or training prepared me for this—uh, *challenge.*"

"God's country, like you said," he reminded her gruffly, jamming his hat back on his head. "But you sure do need help, and that's a fact. I'm going to town now to round up a carpentry crew and some ranch hands.''

She nodded, speechless at the abrupt change in his behavior, his long, drawn-out instructions a far cry from the silent cowboy whose odd, old-fashioned manner was beginning to grow on her and charm her nearly as much as it annoyed her.

Erik turned to go, but then spun on his heels, tipping his hat high on his forehead with the back of his hand. "You *can* pay your help, can't you?"

She laughed shakily at the irony lacing his question.

The church had every penny of their money already budgeted, and she couldn't change a cent of it. She could pay her staff, but couldn't afford to feed herself.

He certainly wouldn't have agreed to work for her if he knew his quarterly bonus horse would come from her own thin-lined pocket. She'd have to take a second job or skimp on necessities, maybe even on her own horse, at least for a while. She wasn't about to tell him *that*.

As much as it infuriated her, he had a definite right to ask about salary, seeing as he was her first official employee.

Was he afraid she wouldn't pay him his wages?

"Of course I'll pay my staff," she snapped, unable to keep exasperation from sounding in her voice. "The church has earmarked funds just for that purpose."

Erik must think her the worst kind of fool. How could he understand the passion she felt for the Lord's work, the One asking her to trust what she couldn't see? And that was nothing to say of the inner workings of church committees.

By his own admittance, he wasn't even a Christian, and even some mature, long-term Christians had trouble with the church committee part.

Either he chose to ignore her tone, or he didn't hear it. "Good thing," he said with a nod. "I wouldn't make a commitment to my men without the money to back my mouth up with."

No, he certainly didn't take his words lightly, she reflected sardonically. Not in any context.

She supposed his reluctance to speak should be considered a virtue, if the book of James had any bearing on it. But in Erik, his *virtue* appeared as a liability, and it rubbed her the wrong way.

Especially the fact that whenever he spoke, he always seemed to be right. That tendency bothered her most of all.

What an annoying habit.

Erik arrived back at the retreat center a little more than four hours later. A tall, barrel-chested man with salt-and-pepper hair that touched his shoulders and a long, matching untrimmed beard accompanied him. The big man's frayed red flannel shirt strained at the seams of his shoulders. Even the strength of his stride was impressive.

Or was that oppressive?

Dixie took a mental step backward. The man looked like a bear, or at least what she thought a bear must look like, being that she'd never seen a live one except in a zoo.

She grimaced as she recalled last night's ruckus with the raccoon and wondered if the huge tree trunk could sense her discomposure. She struggled in vain to fight her emotions.

Even if the grizzly of a man didn't feel her confusion, she was certain Erik saw everything, even the faint flush to her cheeks. He didn't show it, though. Not a muscle moved out of place on his face. Not even his eyes gave him away.

"Dixie, I'd like you to meet Ed McDonnell, your new construction foreman."

The big man grinned and stuck out his hand. "It's a pleasure to meet you, ma'am."

That Dixie caught her jaw before it hit the floor was a feat in itself; that she managed to shake Ed's hand and murmur something intelligible proved that miracles really did happen.

The walking grizzly had the impeccable manners and speech of a Southern gentleman!

She slid a glance at Erik, who had at last cracked a grin. He appeared to be enjoying himself, and she wondered for the tiniest inkling of a moment if Erik hadn't spent the entire morning looking for the most backward-looking man in the territory to bring to her. Just to shake her up a bit.

She wouldn't doubt it for a moment.

He probably didn't know about Ed's polished manners before he brought him up here, she thought cuttingly. It kind of ruined the image, took the edge off, in her opinion. She wondered what Erik thought.

She pinched her mouth into a firm, straight line and met Erik's gaze stare for stare. If he was trying to frighten her off, he was going to have to do a lot better than this.

She had God, and God was a great deal larger than Ed McDonnell. She thrust out her right hand and smiled up at the man.

"Glad to meet you, Mr. McDonnell. I'm sure you'll be perfect for the job. A real asset to our staff." She stopped speaking and shifted her gaze to Erik. "I have absolute faith in Erik's judgment."

Erik's heart leapt around like a newborn calf when her gaze met his. Her sparkling blue eyes were full of laughter—and challenge—neither of which he could figure.

But then again, he'd never claimed to be an expert on women. He'd brought her the best carpenter in South Dakota, as far as he knew. How could she find fault with that?

Besides that, Ed McDonnell was a vocal Christian

influence in Custer, attending church as often as the doors were opened. So what was the problem?

He sent Ed to survey the property, claiming they'd catch up with him in a minute. He might not know women, but he was relatively positive Dixie had a few words for him, and he might as well get it over with.

Impossible woman.

"I will not be intimidated, Mr. Wheeler," she ground out sharply as soon as Ed was out of hearing range.

One thing he was learning about Dixie—she called him *Mr. Wheeler* when she was angry. Clearly, he'd done something to upset her, whatever that might be. He had no clue. But he sure as shootin' had done something wrong.

At least in her mind he had.

"What?" he snapped back, feeling just as prickly as she looked.

"What did you do, spend all morning looking for the biggest man in the county?"

The biggest man…?

"What?" he asked again, rubbing a hand across his jaw. The woman made less than no sense. "The *biggest* man? I brought you the *best* man in the whole county. Isn't that what you wanted?"

"Oh, right. I see. And you're going to stand there and tell me size had nothing to do with your selection."

She marched up to him, planted her clenched fists on her hips and thrust her chin in the air as their gazes met and locked.

At six-foot-even, Erik towered over Dixie. Goliath to the Biblical David, if he remembered his childhood stories from Sunday school.

She was a petite little thing, that's for sure. But she sure did pack a punch.

And then it struck him right between the eyes. He knew what had her so riled up. She thought he'd picked Ed McDonnell to frighten her off.

She couldn't be more wrong.

He pressed his lips together and tugged down on his cowboy hat. He'd never do anything so low, even if he did believe she didn't belong here.

And for some reason, it really bothered him that she thought he was capable of such an act. He'd already decided he wanted her to stick around for a while. But just until he got his colt and filly, of course.

"I'm going to join Ed now," he stated gruffly.

She placed a hand on his arm and he froze, inside and out. Even his lungs refused to work.

"Oh, no, you're not. Not until you assure me Ed McDonnell can do the job. I'm not paying men to intimidate me."

Erik pulled his arm away and glared down at her until the rim of his hat was touching her forehead.

Blood pounded in his head, which felt like an entire continent of oil drummers playing their song.

"Listen up, and listen good," he said, his voice low and gravelly. "Because I'm only going to say this once."

She didn't so much as blink, though her bottom lip quivered slightly, no doubt from anger.

He pulled in a deep, calming breath and continued, though what he really wanted to do was turn and walk away. Or maybe kiss some sense into her. She didn't look like she'd been kissed much. And she should be.

He shook his head. Only the thought of that colt and filly stopped him from doing something irrational—or maybe that was rational. And then just barely.

"I wouldn't hire someone who couldn't do the job," he said in a low monotone, struggling to keep his anger under wraps. "Not even for you."

Chapter Seven

Maybe she'd made a mistake, but he didn't have to get so huffy about it.

Okay, so he'd been right. Again.

A mere week had proven to Dixie the big grizzly named Ed McDonnell was a teddy bear inside, and the month that followed only served to further justify Erik's choice in a foreman. Not only that, but Ed had a faith to rock mountains, and praised the name of Jesus loud and clear every chance he got.

She liked him. She really did.

And, she had to admit, if only to herself, he was an excellent foreman. Under Erik's direction, he'd hand-picked a friendly, hardworking crew of five, all Christians, who'd cleared the messy building area within the first week and had laid the foundation for the new buildings within a month.

She was impressed. Thank the Lord. God was obviously providing for her despite her many setbacks.

Sometimes she wondered if she was deluding herself. But not now.

The carpenters worked not only swiftly, but cheerfully, as well. Each of them had a smile and a pleasant greeting for her when she was around, sweeping off their variety of cowboy hats and calling her *Miz Sullivan,* to her delight.

Men in Denver had never treated her so well, not with half the respect or graciousness these rough-around-the-edges country gentlemen showed. And carpenters in Denver did *not* wear cowboy hats.

Over the course of the first couple of weeks, she'd shed her designer jeans for a pair of Wrangler jeans and tied her hair back in a ponytail. She could almost pass as one of the carpenters, as much dust and mud clung to her by the end of each day.

The most laughable part of it was the pair of boots Erik bought her. She'd been mortified to wear them at first, as unfashionable as they were. But once they were broken in, she couldn't imagine wearing anything else. They molded perfectly to her feet like a second skin. Why hadn't anyone ever told her how comfortable a pair of cowboy boots could be?

Maybe she should announce it to the world and start a new fashion trend. It would be the first time in a long time fashion was actually *comfortable.* She laughed at the thought. She'd changed so much in such a short time, and she didn't regret any of it.

After that first night, sleeping out in a tent didn't bother her as much, especially after Erik fixed the tent so it wasn't liable to fall over should a faint breeze occur some evening.

It had taken a while, but she found she enjoyed living out of a tent, staying outside late, lying out in the dark with so many, many stars twinkling down on her, far more than she'd seen in Colorado with the city lights of Denver blotting them out.

She had her food supply in tough plastic containers—and she now knew not to eat in or near her tent lest animals catch wind of it and think *she* was dinner—and the faithful Border collie who appeared as if by magic every night. She didn't know where the dog came from or where she went afterward, but every night like clockwork, the Border collie returned to guard over her.

She'd managed to cope.

No. Much more than cope. *Live.*

She was thriving, healthy and flourishing on the inside and out, more than she could ever have imagined or hoped for.

She put her management skills to work, as well. The first day the carpentry crew arrived, she'd set out to work right beside them. She wasn't going to be the type of manager who ruled the roost without getting her feathers dirty.

She wanted more than just a working crew. She wanted to create a family atmosphere, and most of all, a peaceful, Christian atmosphere.

And she could only do that by giving it everything she had. She helped out whenever possible, though much of the work was beyond her ability and expertise.

She hauled wood and water, held up poles and learned to sand wood, and cooked and served the men their evening meal.

Okay, so cooking over an open fire wasn't exactly her forte, along with so many other skills she was only now beginning to discover. Flames were tricky things, and she'd burned the fare more than once, though no one had complained.

Erik had laughingly mentioned bringing in a cook to handle that aspect of the job, and soon.

She didn't know whether to be relieved or insulted, though she knew he was only teasing. And it was a rare occasion when Erik said even that much, so she supposed she should be grateful.

The stable was the first building raised, and Erik soon had it filled with horses and a stable crew working under him, forging mountain trails for future visitors and training the gentle horses to trail ride nose to tail, regardless of the equestrian skill— or lack of—in their riders.

She'd been so busy with the plans and construction of the main lodge, she hadn't had time to get down to the barn and greet her new staff. She was anxious to introduce herself and her goals, but quickly discovered the stable hands weren't nearly as anxious to meet her.

"We don't take orders from a *woman*," growled the first stable hand she approached. He had greasy, straw-colored hair and an attitude, Dixie noted, as he crossed his arms over an adolescent-thin chest.

The other four boys followed the young man's lead, crowding in around him and nodding vigorously.

"I beg your pardon?" Dixie blundered, stunned by his rudeness and the blatant animosity on the expressions of the stable hands. The group's unofficial leader pronounced the word *woman* as if it were spoiled food.

"You heard me." The young man spat on the ground by her feet, and it took every bit of her will not to react.

She rankled inside, prickling from head to toe, but other than making a conscious effort to pull herself to her full height, she didn't allow her emotions to show.

She might be hurt and angry at their hostility toward her, but she'd die before she'd show it. She had been caught off guard, expecting the stable hands to show the same friendly attitude as the carpenters.

Mentally retreating a few steps, she looked the

group over. Every one of them looked uncomfortable, and the leader downright hostile.

They were testing her, she realized, like a toddler tested his mother's limits. She definitely wasn't expecting a brash confrontation after experiencing the easy nature of the construction crew, and she struggled to adjust to this new curve thrown at her.

Maybe part of her training should have included working with a youth group, she thought, however belated the realization. She should have known most of her staff would be youngsters.

She knew if she backed down now, the fight would be over. She had to confront this hostility head-on, nip it in the bud so it didn't grow and spread.

"Am I correct in assuming that when Mr. Wheeler hired you on, it was with the understanding that you work for *me?*" she asked bluntly.

"We answer to Wheeler," the belligerent ringleader retorted, drawling his words.

"You'll answer to me," she snapped back, unable to contain the sting of rejection a moment longer. She'd felt it too many times in the past to put up with it now, especially from a gaggle of adolescent boys.

She pinned each of them with a glare in turn, especially the straw-haired boy. "Them's the rules, boys. If you don't like it, feel free to walk. But if you're going to quit, do it now. I don't expect to hear about this again. Understood?"

She whirled in place, her form-fitting boots stirring a cloud of dust around her feet. She had to get out of there, and fast, before she flew off the handle and told the boys what she really thought of their adolescent behavior.

She sent up a frantic prayer for help to contain the fury pounding through her, the nearly overwhelming need to vocalize her opinion of their prehistoric, chauvinistic attitudes.

She wanted them to know they were pushing her personal buttons—and that she wasn't about to put up with it.

What she really wanted was to fire the whole lot of them, right here and now.

The only thing keeping her from doing that very thing was the knowledge Erik handpicked each man for the stable, and their individual abilities with horses. Each of these men excelled in their skills. They must, if Erik chose them.

He must believe they'd be able to handle the guests of a *Christian* retreat, even if she disagreed at the moment. The least she could do was consult him first, before firing the whole lot of them and forcing Erik back to square one.

She might be making a lion's share of mistakes, but Dixie Sullivan never made the same mistake twice.

She'd accused Erik of trying to run her off when he'd brought her the big grizzly of a carpentry foreman, but she knew better now. She wouldn't throw the stable hands' attitudes in his face.

In fact, she wasn't certain she would mention the incident to him at all. Wasn't she the one insisting he didn't help her out of every jam? She'd have to figure out an answer to this dilemma on her own.

Erik had his reasons for what he did and the men he hired, though he rarely spoke about them, or about anything else, for that matter. He'd given her no reason to distrust him up to this point, and she believed he'd do what he thought best for her—for the retreat, she mentally amended.

For some reason, he'd hired these particular boys to run the stable, although at the moment, she couldn't imagine why.

Their crude, repellent behavior worried her. If they were this rude to her, how could she ever hope they'd lead pleasant trail rides for her guests, those who came to relax and find God here? Didn't they understand they were working for a *Christian* retreat center?

Evidently not. Or else they just didn't care. She'd have to figure out what to do, and soon.

As she stomped away, she overheard the boys taking turns letting out a string of mockery. She froze, their scornful words ringing in her ears. She clenched her fists to keep from turning around and letting them have it with all the fury of a hurricane.

She'd have a talk with them, all right.

But not right now. Not here, on their turf, in their time. She was sharp enough to realize they had her at a disadvantage here, catching her off guard as they had.

She needed time to think. She had to be in control of the situation—and her emotions—if she was ever going to convince them to cooperate, and right now she knew she'd do little more than yell and throw insults back at them. Which would just prove their point—that she was an irrational, emotional female incapable of running this retreat.

And she needed time to pray about it.

Apprehension and uncertainty washed over her, emotions that had become more and more familiar to her as the days passed.

Maybe the stable hands were right. Maybe she couldn't do it alone. Hadn't Erik said the very same thing?

Frowning, she blew out a breath and continued walking toward the safety and privacy of her truck. Maybe the boys were just testing her. If that were so, she'd pass the test and win their trust.

If not, they'd be the ones to go, not her.

Wild animals weren't going to scare her away from doing the Lord's work here in South Dakota, and neither was a pack of feral stable hands.

Come what may, she was determined to make this retreat center a reality.

Erik stepped farther into the shadow of the stable as Dixie walked by. She looked ready to spontaneously combust, and with good reason.

He'd been standing in the shadows since the beginning of the confrontation, hearing and seeing everything that transpired between Dixie and the stable hands.

Admiration for Dixie's courage raged with fury for the boys' brutal treatment of her. He'd been genuinely surprised when she stood up to the ignorant, ill-mannered adolescents—and not only stood up to them, but talked them down to size.

Dixie Sullivan might be short of stature, but she was in no way short of spirit.

He wondered, and not for the first time since he'd met her, about the reserve she drew on, the mysterious way she found strength beyond her measure.

Naturally she attributed it to God.

God doing the real work here. God leading the way through every path, both rough and smooth. God infusing her with the strength and courage to continue, when any sane person would quit and go home.

But to Erik, her words were nothing more than a mouthful of gibberish, completely useless in the real world. Dixie used God as a crutch because she didn't have enough confidence in her own ability. She didn't see the many things she accomplished all on her own.

Did she think just *any* woman could wander off in the wilderness on her own with dreams as big as castles, and actually have any hope of making those dreams a reality?

Most people wouldn't even dare to dream.

And where reality was concerned, Dixie herself was doing most of the work. God wasn't giving her any breaks, either, as far as Erik was concerned.

If anything, He was pitching her one challenge after another. Nothing Dixie attempted came as easily as it could. Or should.

Not if God, this personal God full of love and mercy, this God who supposedly communed one-on-one with His subjects—*really* wanted to help. It sure wasn't for lack of trying on Dixie's part.

He didn't understand Christians' faith, though he respected them, since his mother had been one of the faithful. But she had died young. His father withdrew, leaving Erik and his brothers virtual orphans.

His father. The poster child of hypocrites. He'd never believed, but then, when he died, he left his ranch, the only thing he *hadn't* neglected, to Erik's mother's church.

It was Erik's birthright. He'd worked right along with his father. Everyone expected the ranch to be his one day.

Instead, he'd been left with nothing.

He pounded his fist into the corner post on the stable wall. God wasn't there to help then. Why should He be here now?

God might not be here to help Dixie out with her problems, but Erik was, and he was of a mind to help her himself. He could—*would*—do something about those stupid, ignorant fools. They had a lot to learn about how to treat a lady.

Especially a lady boss.

He adjusted his hat low over his eyes and stepped out of the shadows, marching decisively toward the stable boys with a frown on his face. He had a few choice words for each of them, and each word was going to hurt like the dickens.

But they were going to hear him out until he was sure they got the message. *Loud and clear.*

The only reason he hadn't intervened when they challenged Dixie was that he didn't want to undermine her authority, not to mention her confidence in herself, by taking over. He recognized her volatility, and how threatened she was when he tried to help her, however well-intentioned his efforts.

But the men needed to understand who held the reins in this particular operation.

Dixie Sullivan.

And now that Dixie wasn't around, he was going to make good and sure the stable hands weren't laboring under any misconceptions.

"Ellis," he barked at the belligerent cowboy. "You and the rest of the men, front and center. Now."

He leaned both elbows against the rough-hewn wood of the newly fashioned corral fence and waited, knowing the men would comply.

As he expected, as unjust as it was, the stable hands immediately left the tasks they'd been attending after their confrontation with Dixie and gathered around him, their expressions intent and respectful.

Erik's fists begged to speak louder than his voice, but he clenched and unclenched his hands until the itch to do physical harm passed. He wasn't going to roughhouse them unless necessary, but he wouldn't hesitate if they balked against what he had to say. He'd dealt with stubborn calves before.

If the boys thought they could treat Dixie like some kind of department store mannequin, and then turn around and muster up to Erik like nothing was wrong, just because he was a man, they had another think coming.

Loud and clear.

"I understand you men gave Miss Sullivan a hard time."

A scowl of annoyance creased Ellis's face. "What'd she do, go crying to you, boss?" He barked a laugh and chucked Erik on the arm. "Just like a woman to go all to pieces, ain't it?"

The other boys snickered, until Erik stopped them

short with a single look. They sobered immediately, looking contrite and uncomfortable, except for Ellis, who looked as if he were ready for a fight.

"Let's get one thing straight," Erik ground out, eyeing each man in turn, and at last resting and holding his gaze on Ellis. "Miss Sullivan is your employer. And she's also a lady. You'll treat her with due respect as *both*—your boss lady."

The boys nodded, wide-eyed with apprehension.

All except Ellis, who grunted skeptically. "I don't take no orders from—"

"That means," Erik interrupted, not allowing the younger man to finish, "you will remove your hat in her presence, speak to her quietly and with respect, and you will do exactly what she tells you to do. Without complaining. Is that clear?"

Again, four of the boys nodded.

"Ellis?" he challenged, his pulse pounding in his ears. If the young man was itching for a fight, he was going to get more than he bargained for.

The young man shrugged and glared over Erik's shoulder, murmuring something incomprehensible under his breath.

"And if I ever hear foul language coming from any of you—at any time, on- or off-duty—you'll be history. This is a Christian retreat. Respect that fact or pack your bags and git."

He met each man's eyes one last time, then turned

away. The urge to hit something still pulsed through him, barely restrained by the strength of his will.

He'd scarcely gone two steps when Ellis began complaining loudly to the other cowboys about the unfair working conditions they were under.

Erik bristled but walked away, allowing the young man to vent to his own satisfaction. The battle wasn't over, not by a long shot.

Ellis was a troublemaker, and he knew beyond a doubt there would be a one-on-one confrontation between him and the boy before long.

If Ellis didn't force it, Erik would.

But however it happened, he wanted to keep Dixie out of the middle of it. She wouldn't stand down from today's challenge, and she'd be furious if she knew Erik had reinforced her battlements without her knowledge.

He still wasn't sure why, but he already knew Dixie's pet peeves. Funny. He hadn't known her that long, but he already felt he knew her better than anyone he'd known in a good, long time. Maybe ever.

And maybe one day he would learn why she was so desperate to prove her independence.

She'd step right up to the plate if she had the opportunity, and fight back with all she was worth.

Which meant he had to make sure she didn't get that opportunity.

He'd have to be extra watchful and on his guard,

to make sure nothing happened between Dixie and Ellis before he got to the belligerent young man first.

He didn't want to examine the fierce need to protect Dixie. She was an obligation and nothing more. Ellis was his responsibility, since he'd brought the loud-mouthed boy on board as a stable hand.

Ellis was his responsibility and his problem.

He probably ought to have fired him right off, but he was afraid the other boys would walk, as well, out of loyalty to Ellis, which would leave him in the lurch.

There wasn't time to find another crew and get the needed work done before the first guests arrived in a little over two months. He needed every second, and every man, to finish this project on time.

But Ellis was going to be a detriment to the work by staying on, and there was no getting around it. The boy was an uncouth, loudmouthed brat. With his childish attitude, he ought to be in the nursery, not running horses.

He'd come with references, but obviously from people who didn't care what the young man said or did as long as he got his work done.

And until Dixie entered the picture, Ellis had been working hard. Now Erik doubted he'd get a good day's work from the boy.

And he didn't even want to think about Dixie and Ellis in a showdown. His insides stung as if a hive of killer bees had been let loose in his stomach.

Ellis was just stupid enough to push Dixie beyond her limit. She was a strong woman, but Erik didn't want to be there when she *really* exploded. Erik had a feeling a tornado would be safer to watch.

A showdown between Dixie and Ellis wasn't a possibility he cared to consider. But it wasn't going to happen. Not if he was here to stop it.

And he was.

Chapter Eight

After what felt to Dixie like a lifetime, but was in reality only six weeks from the day she stepped onto South Dakota soil, acquiring a horse of her own was finally, wonderfully, joyfully next on her list.

She'd been up to her ears in construction and renovation, overseeing a stable of horses for the ministry, hiring a kitchen and housekeeping staff, moving into her own small studio in the main lodge and avoiding the stable hands like the plague.

She was physically and emotionally exhausted from the whole ordeal, as much from all the blessings God showered her with as much as from the challenges she continued to encounter.

Erik suggested a day off, and she'd finally concurred. She hadn't had a break since she'd started, other than the occasional peach-scented bubble bath in her new studio.

So this sunshine-filled Saturday morning, she'd called some phone numbers in the newspaper and set up appointments to see if she could find *her* horse.

She wasn't a complete novice where horses were concerned, she thought with pride. That is to say, she'd ridden a horse a few times as a kid, and had been told even then that she was a natural horsewoman.

And she'd read every *How to Take Care of a Horse of Your Own* book the Denver Public Library possessed, up to and including the children's books.

She was relatively certain she could groom, tack and mount her horse. It couldn't possibly be any worse than the rivers she'd forged thus far in her pioneer journey.

All she needed was the horse to prove it.

Her heart raced with anticipation as she drove off the compound. She was especially looking forward to her first stop, a man named Needleson. He was her nearest neighbor with the exception of Erik. Needleson owned a large spread that bordered her own on two sides. From what she knew of him, his was one of, if not *the* most prosperous ranches in the area.

It would be good to finally meet her neighbors. Solitude was wonderful, up to a point, but she looked forward to getting to know others in Custer, most especially those who lived near her retreat. She'd just been too busy lately to seek out fellowship, other than on Sundays in a small Custer church.

Did John Needleson have a wife and kids? Would they be Christians?

She hoped so. Maybe they could be friends, get together for a cookout and perhaps even have a Bible study. She could offer the services of her retreat, once it was up and running, if they wanted a break from ranching.

She only realized how far distant her daydreams had taken her when she noted the large Bar N sign that indicated the entrance to the Needleson ranch. Laughing merrily at herself, she turned onto the Bar N road, noting it had the same bumpy washboard consistency as her own dirt road.

John Needleson said he'd be waiting for her in front of his stable with the horse he had in mind for her. He'd almost sounded excited when he told her about the feisty brown-and-white Appaloosa gelding.

She couldn't help but allow his enthusiasm to raise her hopes. Wouldn't it be lovely if the first horse she "shopped" for was the right one?

She shook her head and chuckled. There she went again, daydreaming in a very real world, where daydreams could be dangerous.

A fiftyish-looking man with white tufts of hair that stuck up in every direction on his head waited for her outside his very large, very modern-looking stable. She didn't notice another thing about him, except that he was holding on to the most beautiful horse she'd ever seen.

She had looked at a million pictures of horses in books and on-line, but the one before her beat them all in looks and style.

She quickly parked her truck and rushed to the horse's side, not caring that her anticipation and delight were showing. John Needleson had been right on the mark for her in choosing a horse.

Her heart pounded as she looked the gelding over. The Appaloosa tossed his head as if protesting the halter he wore, then whickered softly.

He was spirited, she realized, which enchanted her almost as much as his wavy mane. Equally attractive was the gentle nature of his eyes as he nuzzled her hand, looking for a treat.

"He's a fine horse, ma'am," said Mr. Needleson, speaking for the first time. "As soon as I spoke with you on the telephone, I just had a feeling this young fellow was the one you were looking for."

Startled, she remembered her manners. "I beg your pardon, Mr. Needleson. I'm Dixie Sullivan, your new neighbor."

The man smiled, but for some reason it didn't appear to reach his eyes. He looked rough and hard, but she supposed career cowboys would look that way. Perhaps she was judging too harshly.

"John will do, ma'am."

She reached out her hand, determination to make him her friend welling up in her. "And of course you'll call me Dixie."

He mumbled something under his breath and nodded, directing his gaze to the horse.

She didn't need any prodding to turn her attention back to the horse. "I'm sure you noticed how charmed I am by your pony. He is everything I've ever dreamed of."

John chuckled. She snapped her gaze to his, but his eyes were shaded. Was he laughing at her?

She felt heat rise to her face, knowing she was showing far more enthusiasm than she should, as the buyer. She wondered if buying horses was like buying cars, where only a fool paid the full price.

But this horse, which she'd already mentally named Victory, was worth whatever price she paid. Besides, the price John named was reasonable. Cheap, even, if the ads she'd perused were anything to go by.

"How many horses have you seen this morning, Miss Sullivan?" John drawled, running a rough hand through the chaotic tips of his hair.

She noted he clung to formality. She hoped it didn't mean he distrusted her, or wouldn't be willing to sell Victory to her.

"To be honest, Victory—I mean, your gelding—is the first horse I've looked at," she admitted. "I suppose I ought to see the rest of the horses on my list before I make my final decision."

She already knew she'd choose Victory, no matter how many other horses she saw today or any day. She was decisive, and that's how it went when she had her heart set on something.

Still, she thought she probably ought to go through the motion of shopping around, at least, in case anyone asked her.

"Nonsense," John replied promptly. "You don't buy a horse like you buy clothes or groceries or something." He thumped his chest with his fist. "It's a heart thing."

A heart thing.

An odd idea to come from a tough cowboy like John. There must be more to the man than what appeared on the surface, she decided, her heart discerning a story underneath his words he wasn't willing to share.

In any case, John was right. It *was* a heart thing. She could feel it—she and Victory were meant to be together. Like peanut butter and jelly.

She ran her hands over the horse, noticing once again how skittish he was around his head and legs. But John quickly explained that away, saying he was still young and not used to strangers. That was probably all there was to it. Surely nothing out of the ordinary.

John walked the gelding around the corral a couple of times, allowing her to look him over. He had a nice, easy gait, pleasant to the eyes. He would be a joy to ride, she just knew it.

"Is he what you're looking for?" John asked when she didn't speak. "I don't mean to sound pushy, but as it happens, I've got another buyer who is extremely interested in this gelding. He's coming by this afternoon, in fact. I'll let you have first dibs at this fine fellow, but I can't hold him for you until you make a decision. I hope you understand."

She nodded, then mentally faltered. Faking another buyer was the oldest salesman trick in the book. Was she being conned by this sweet yet gruff old man?

"I think I'd..." She wished she'd invited Erik along. He'd know for sure if she was making a wise choice.

She didn't even know what other questions to ask, what else to check out, other than his gait and any obvious outward faults.

Erik would know.

Should she ask to ride the horse before she bought him? What if Victory had some inward, hidden fault she couldn't see with the naked eye? Something a true horseman like Erik would recognize.

"I wondered if I could—or you, I guess—could ride him for a minute?"

John immediately shook his head. "Sorry, ma'am. Can't do."

He lifted up one of Victory's legs, slapping the horse on the neck when he shied away. Gripping Victory's leg between his knees, he pointed to the bottom of the hoof. "He's not shod. You'll have to have that done before you can ride him."

"Oh." She was both disappointed and embarrassed at not knowing better. A real horsewoman would know such things.

Heat flared to her cheeks as she mentally stammered over what to say next.

But then she realized it didn't matter whether or not she rode the horse now, or even whether there might be some sort of fault with him. Even if she never once rode this horse in her lifetime, he was *her* horse.

She'd have him shod this afternoon, and then she'd learn to ride him, no matter what quirks he might have. Even if it took her a year to become proficient in the basics.

It didn't matter. She already felt a growing love for Victory, and sensed instinctively he would return the affection she gave.

Since she didn't bring Erik to check the horse out, she'd have to follow her heart on this one and trust in God for the rest.

Maybe it was foolish, but there it was. She'd waited her whole life for this moment.

"I want to buy him."

Her heart lightened the moment the words were out of her mouth. Everything was going to work out. It had to. God had brought her this far. He wasn't going to let her down now, not with the fulfillment of a lifelong dream right here in front of her.

John smiled, this time the genuine article. He looked years younger, the hard lines on his face fading.

"What does Mrs. Needleson think of this beauty?" she asked, lightly probing about his personal life.

His mouth immediately became a thin, hard line that matched the ice in his gaze. She sighed inwardly, wishing she'd kept her big mouth shut and left well enough alone. But she was only trying to be neighborly.

"I'm sorry. I shouldn't have—"

"It's okay," he said gruffly, interrupting her apology with a wave. "Cathy died two years ago. This is her mare's foal."

"I'm sorry," she said again. "Really." Her heart broke for the man. He obviously missed his wife desperately. Even the birth of his wife's mare's foal brought back painful memories.

She reached out, placing a gentle hand on his

forearm, wanting to lend whatever small comfort she could. "It must be very hard for you."

He snatched his arm away and glared at her. "It's okay. Now, do you want this horse or don't you?"

She opened her mouth to speak, but her throat was dry.

Raising one eyebrow, he looked at his watch and shrugged.

Dixie decided to ignore his harsh tone and narrow attitude, writing it off as inner pain he wasn't ready to deal with. It was only natural he'd have misgivings when faced with so many tender memories.

"I'd like to buy your horse. And I can promise you he'll have a wonderful new home with me. I have lots of land, and a wonderful new stable to house him in."

John snorted. "Yeah. A wonderful new home."

Dixie pulled her hard-earned money from her pocket and counted out the crisp, new hundred-dollar bills with shaking fingers. "I'll have one of my stable hands pick him up this afternoon."

He took the money and pocketed it without looking at her. "Got yourself a real nice spread over there, do you?" The words were angry, derisive.

She raised her eyebrows in surprise. "Very. I hope you'll visit sometime."

She made the offer without expecting him to hear the words, never mind respond.

He grunted. "I'll do that."

She looked up at him, taken aback by his casual statement. "You will?"

"Believe me, Miss Sullivan, you can bank on it."

Chapter Nine

Erik sent his two most reliable men—definitely *not* including Ellis—to pick up Dixie's new horse and have him shod in town as she'd instructed.

She had surprised him with her declaration that she'd *found the one,* as if choosing a horse was some kind of magical heart thing, and not knowledge and logic.

It wasn't all knowledge and logic for him, either, he supposed. More of a gut instinct.

But then again, *he* knew what he was doing. Dixie was a complete novice where horses were concerned.

And she'd named him Victory.

He chuckled aloud and shook his head. What kind of a name was that for a horse?

The stable boys arrived back, bounding out of the

truck with the energy of youth. But instead of going to unload the horse, they made a beeline straight for him, their expressions sober.

Worried.

"What's wrong?" he muttered, immediately sensing trouble.

"It's Miz Sullivan's new horse, boss," the older of the two hands answered, pulling his hat off and mopping his forehead with his sleeve. "He's—"

"What?"

"Well. Would you look at this." Erik recognized the sarcastic drawl as Ellis's, and it was coming from the back of the trailer.

He gestured to the two youths, his gaze warning them to get Ellis away from the horse and out of the picture before Dixie arrived. It was no secret how Erik felt about Ellis, and how Ellis felt about Dixie. Everyone involved knew of the animosity between the threesome.

He set off immediately behind the stable hands, his heart bolting out of his chest as he saw Dixie rounding the corner of the main lodge, her eyes sparkling in delight.

He made an abrupt turn to intercept her, hoping to allow the hands time to deal with Ellis.

"Did you see Victory yet?" she asked, bouncing with nervous energy. She reached for his hand and pulled him along, as eager as a young child to show off her prize.

"Not yet," he answered gruffly, but he didn't release her hand, which felt soft and tiny in his. He allowed her to drag him, as slowly as he could manage, in the direction of the trailer.

"What a hoot." Ellis again. Apparently the hands hadn't done their job.

"What?" Dixie demanded, dropping Erik's hand and rounding the corner of the trailer to confront Ellis. "What's wrong with Victory?"

Ellis barked out a laugh. "You don't know, do you, little miss?"

Erik felt darkness drop over him like a cloak. With supreme effort, he managed to control his anger, and with even less restraint, his fist, which clenched convulsively, begging for a target.

"Ellis," he warned, his voice low and gravelly.

"What, boss?" Ellis protested. "I was just looking over Victory here," he said, snickering as he said the horse's name. "A fine-looking horse she's got here. Perfect for her."

Erik frowned at Ellis, then turned his attention to Victory, his gaze automatically running over the gelding's frame, checking him for faults from head to toe.

He was a real beauty of a horse, all right. Erik would have chosen Victory himself, if given the opportunity.

But for Dixie?

Not the choice he would have made. Not the kind

of horse he'd pictured her riding. Not the sweet, gentle mare he'd put her on.

He knew without asking exactly to what Ellis was referring. The horse was skittering way too much under a simple rope halter lead, and his round, brown eyes communicated his panic.

"Lady, you can't ride this horse," Ellis declared, hooting his disdain.

Dixie planted her fists on her hips and frowned. "And why is that, exactly?"

Erik's chest tightened as he stepped forward to intercept the impending storm. She looked so tough. And inside she was so very vulnerable.

Why hadn't she taken him with her to buy a horse? She should have asked for his help. He would have gladly given it to her.

"For starters," Ellis sneered, "because he's green broke and newly gelded. Don't tell me you didn't know that."

"So?" she demanded, her face turning a shade darker by the second.

"Did you ride him, Dixie?" Erik asked gently, quietly, attempting to turn the tide of the conversation.

She whirled on him, her eyes glowing with sparks of anger that made his gut clench in empathy. "No, of course I didn't ride him. He didn't have his shoes on yet, as you well know."

This time, every one of the stable hands laughed,

though they sobered immediately when faced with Erik's glare.

He reached for her, but she backed away and folded her arms around herself in an instinctively protective gesture that made Erik's heart ache for her.

"What?" she asked, sounding suspicious as her gaze darted from boy to boy, finally resting on Ellis. "What did I do wrong?"

He wished she wouldn't have phrased her question that way, especially not while looking straight at Ellis. She was unconsciously blaming herself for her error, even before she knew what she'd actually done wrong.

And Ellis was the worst person in the world she could ask. Couldn't she see the blatant animosity spewing from the young man?

"You've been had, lady. You can't ride this horse," the belligerent boy scoffed.

"That'll be enough, Ellis," Erik barked.

Dixie laid a gentle hand on Erik's chest, causing his heart to stop cold. "It's okay, Erik. Let him have his say." And to Ellis, "Go on."

"You shouldn't buy a horse without riding him," he instructed, looking superior.

"I told you, I—"

"You can ride a horse without shoeing him first, Dixie. Especially in the meadow," Erik inserted, his voice low and gentle, the same tone he'd use with the skittish horse now tied to the trailer.

"But John said I couldn't!"

"John?" he asked, puzzled.

"John Needleson."

Her nearest neighbor, discounting Erik.

Erik tensed. There was something more going on here than merely a mistake. It was a gut feeling, but he was a man who paid attention to his instincts.

He shook his head, though he kept his thoughts to himself. He'd bet his next paycheck Needleson sold her a green broke horse on purpose. He'd flat-out lied to her, and Erik wanted to know why. He made a mental note to investigate—find out just exactly what John Needleson was up to, and why he had any negative interest in Dixie.

"How could I have known horses didn't need shoes?" Dixie's eyes welled with tears, and Erik had never felt so helpless as he did at that moment. "Humans do."

You could have taken me with you, he wanted to yell, but instead he put an arm around her. "It was an honest mistake," he soothed.

Every tear wounded him, and he couldn't imagine what they were doing to her. He only wished he could somehow take away her pain.

Incapable of helping Dixie through her trauma, he refocused his anger on John Needleson. How could the man deceive her like that?

"Snivel a little. That'll help," Ellis taunted, laughing derisively.

"You're *gone,*" Erik shouted, glad he finally had someone to vent on. "As of now."

"You've gotta be kidding!" Ellis yelled, turning on him. "I'm the best man you have to run your horses, and you know it."

"Not anymore you're not," Dixie inserted, wiping her tears away with the edge of her flannel shirt and glaring at Ellis.

Then she turned to Erik, her eyes flaming with anger. "And I don't need your help. I can handle my staff problems on my own."

Ignoring Dixie, Ellis shoved Erik on the shoulder, but he stood his ground. "You're gonna can me because of a *woman?*"

"I'm firing you because of your attitude. Now move." Erik turned his back on the young man and reached for the horse, which warily shifted to the side, away from his grasp.

He immediately dropped his hand and lowered his voice. "The rest of you boys better find something productive to do. Now."

He didn't have to say it twice. They were gone.

But when he turned around, so was Dixie.

Chapter Ten

Dixie had never been so disappointed in her life. Or so humiliated.

She had no one to blame but herself for her actions, and the fingers of guilt pointed right at her. She had bought the first horse she'd seen, and hadn't even had the common sense to mount him.

It was bad enough the entire brood of stable hands had witnessed her error. They already disliked and distrusted her, and now she'd given them plenty of fodder with which to verify their original impressions.

But what distressed her most was seeing the gentle compassion on Erik's face as he commiserated with her over her own stupidity. His tender expression was forever etched in her mind.

If he'd maligned her as the others had done, she

could have handled it, brushed it off and forgotten it happened. But if a picture was worth a thousand words, Erik's expression was worth ten times that.

She didn't know why it mattered so much—why it mattered at all. She'd had her one love, and look how that turned out. She didn't want to think of Erik as a man, especially a man she could depend and lean on. Her heart welled, but she forced her feelings back.

She didn't need a man. What Erik thought didn't matter. But the situation rankled nonetheless, a vaguely familiar feeling from childhood, and from her father.

A sensitive little girl and only child who wanted to please her daddy, she'd felt awful whenever she'd done something wrong, whether intentionally or by accident.

She remembered the stern look on her father's face that said *I'm disappointed in you.*

He never had to say a word to load guilt on her small shoulders. A look would do just as well—better, perhaps, for all that was left unspoken.

She hated rejection, especially from those she most loved.

But she was an adult now, and not a child to be reprimanded. And Erik was as different from her father as night was from day.

He was—well, she didn't know what he was, other than extraordinary.

He'd been a perfect gentleman, not censuring her for her mistake, but sympathizing with her. Why did his compassion load the guilt on so much stronger than if he'd brushed her off or dressed her down?

And why did she care so much what he thought?

The fact of the matter was, she should have asked his advice and she hadn't. She should have allowed him to come with her as an expert horseman, but she hadn't. She'd selfishly wanted to keep this one area of her life to herself alone.

And she'd been wrong.

As an adult she could admit that, and, she realized belatedly, she should. The best thing for her to do now was to find Erik and apologize. Then they'd both feel better.

She'd explain why she had chosen Victory, however irrational her reasons might be, and he'd tell her for sure if she'd made an irreparable mistake.

Finding Erik wouldn't be difficult, she thought fondly. If he wasn't in the dining room, he was in the stable with the horses. His love for horses was one of his most endearing qualities, and Dixie found her stomach fluttering in her throat.

It was only a short walk from her new studio apartment in the main lodge to the barn, and as she walked, she admired the many changes she—*they* had made.

The main lodge, a beautiful, rustic log cabin structure with evergreen trim, was finished, complete with a large kitchen and a staff to match. Individual log cabins for guest facilities were springing up around the outskirts of the main lodge, tucked privately into the profusion of pine trees.

The stable was the delightful centerpiece of the retreat, with well over a dozen trail horses for staff and guests. The stable hands had broken several trails, and had even set up a faux campsite for steak-dinner rides and singing guitar-accompanied hymns around a campfire.

Erik had even promised to teach her to handle a team of horses with the hay wagon. Hayrack rides were one of her favorite childhood memories. She couldn't wait to share the experience with a whole new generation of bright-eyed children.

Abel would be pleased she'd done so well. For some reason, his memory didn't hurt as much. She wasn't lonely anymore.

She had God. And Erik was coming to mean more to her by the day. God had given her a new direction, and she found she was really, truly able to find joy through her sorrow.

She entered the stable, immediately inhaling the pungent, enticing aroma of fresh horse and hay. She loved the inherent peace the stable brought to her soul.

Here, she often thought of Jesus being born in a lowly manger, and grasped a small snippet of understanding of the wisdom of God in sending a King to be born in such a place, swaddled in a bed of hay.

But she was rarely alone in the stable, and was surprised to find no one was present. Not Erik, nor a single one of the stable boys.

"Erik?" She called his name several times, but heard only the echo of her own voice from the rafters in response.

She turned to go, then hesitated. She might not be able to ride Victory, but there was no reason not to visit him and start to build a trust relationship between them.

She could feed him a sugar cube or a carrot, anyway. Maybe even groom him.

She walked down the middle of the stable aisle, noting the nameplates on each of the stalls, some with horses whickering and snorting at her over the doors.

Jazz. Commander. Mercury. Antonio. But where was Victory?

The stable hand nicknamed Tallahassee shuffled noisily through the back door at the opposite end of the stable, which was a normal, human-size door, as opposed to the front, wide-swinging doors specially made to accommodate the horses.

The boy whistled as he worked, and didn't appear to notice Dixie, who stood silently watching him for a moment, a little nervous about speaking to one of the stable hands individually, though of course she'd never show it to his face.

She still didn't understand their aversion to her. Though they treated her with respect, they appeared to avoid her as studiously as she avoided them.

Tally was a sturdy, broadly built boy, and one of the friendlier hands. She felt he'd warmed to her, just a little, but it was hard to tell, especially in the company of his peers, where she usually found him.

Her heart stirred with longing to introduce this boy—each of the boys—to the Lord who loved them.

When Tally looked up and realized he was being watched, he immediately stopped whistling and swept his hat from his head, exposing a mop of shoulder-length golden-brown curls. "Is there something I can do for you, Miz Sullivan?" he asked respectfully.

There was none of the mockery or coarseness on his face or in his voice which she half expected, expressions she'd often experienced in the past.

And Tally had more reason than any to ridicule her, as he was one of the boys sent to get Victory.

He knew all the details of her blunder, probably by heart. But unlike Ellis, he didn't appear inclined to razz her with his superior knowledge and her own foolishness.

"I wonder if you could point me in the direction of Victory's stall."

He nodded, though he looked oddly perplexed at her simple query. "Yes, ma'am, Miz Sullivan."

"Thank you, Tally."

He directed her back down the long double row of stalls, stopping before the stall nearest the front doors. "Right here, ma'am. We haven't made a nameplate for him yet."

"That's okay, Tally." She looked to see if he found the name Victory as amusing as Erik appeared to, but Tally was looking at his boots, his face lightly flushed.

She smiled at the adolescent's shy reaction to her. It beat resentment by a long shot.

"I think I'd like to get him a plate myself. Something unique. Victory is special to me."

Tally nodded, his gaze now fixed on her. She could see he understood the odd, wonderful connection between horse and human. He'd make a good stable hand, when he grew into the job.

She now understood and accepted Erik's choice, at least in Tally. Maybe the other boys were the same. She hoped they'd choose to stay the year, maybe longer.

Anxious to see her beauty boy, she walked up to the stall door, reaching in her pocket for a sugar cube. "Victory isn't here," she exclaimed.

Tally shrugged. "No, ma'am."

At least now she knew why he'd looked so perplexed when she'd asked to see the horse. He'd known Victory wasn't there.

Now why didn't he share that vital shred of information with her?

"Where is he?" she demanded, then instantly regretted her imperious tone. She flashed him an apologetic smile, which he returned with a tentative grin of his own, blushing so strongly, his freckled face looked like it might be sunburned.

He cleared his throat, then toed his boot into the dirt. "Mr. Wheeler has him," he admitted quietly, looking as if he were wishing he could dig a hole to China with his boot and climb on through.

With effort, she restrained the annoyance she felt with Erik for taking her horse without her knowledge, and patted Tally on the shoulder. "I don't suppose you know where he is?"

She forced herself to keep her voice gentle and persuading, though what she really wanted to do was shout the barn down.

Tally looked away.

He obviously didn't want to tell her. She watched a war rage on his face, and she knew what he was thinking. She was the boss lady, but Erik might not care to have his whereabouts known, and most especially not blabbed to the female boss by a common stable hand.

"Never mind, Tally, I'll find him myself," she

said, saving him the agony of a decision. She turned away, toward the back door and the corrals.

"You might look for him in the back pasture," Tally said so low, she almost didn't hear him. She glanced back to see him plant his sweat-stained, honey-colored hat on his head.

She chuckled lightly. "Thanks, Tally."

He tipped his hat and grinned shyly.

She found Erik just where Tally indicated, in the back pasture, with Victory on a long, braided rope. She marched toward the pasture, primed and loaded to read him the riot act, but as she approached and saw what he was doing, she realized she was witnessing something out of the ordinary.

Erik spoke in the same low, kind tone he used with her when they were alone, though she'd never heard such a long string of words from the man's mouth at one time.

Her heart fluttered erratically as she listened, feeling like an eavesdropper. His words were soft and sweet, the words of a lover. She wanted to close her eyes and let the resonance of his voice wrap around her, though she vetoed her heart's content.

Not surprisingly, the horse was responding. How could he not, she wondered, with such a man beckoning?

Victory whickered at the man and paced around him in an easy trot at a distance of several feet. Erik kept the lead loose, guiding the horse with his voice more than his hand.

Dixie found herself responding, as well. If she were a horse, she most certainly would have whickered as Victory had done. Inside, she felt as soft as a down comforter, and knew her reaction was *quite* different than her horse's reaction, whicker or not.

She watched for a moment more, then suddenly felt she was intruding on a private moment between horse and man. She spent an awkward second wondering what she should do.

Leave or stay?

In the end, she didn't announce her presence. Neither did she leave, though her conscience pricked her that she ought to. But her eyes were glued to the silent dance and her heart compelled her to stay and watch.

Erik stopped crooning, and the horse stopped pacing. Victory froze, muscles taut and gloriously alert, his uneven mane waving in the gentle mountain wind.

Erik was equally still, his gaze calmly resting on the horse, which eyed him speculatively but without fear.

He didn't say a word, but Dixie couldn't erase the impression he communicated with Victory, something beyond what she could hear, something far beyond the scheme of normal horse-human contact.

She pulled a breath and held it, biting the corner of her lip as a silent reminder not to make a sound.

After several minutes, Erik made a horselike nicker and lifted a hand toward Victory. Dixie expected the skittish yearling to bolt, but to her astonishment and delight, he responded to the invitation, moving forward and nudging Erik's hand, sniffing around his pockets for a tasty treat.

"That's it, Vic, my man," Erik encouraged, sounding pleased. "That's my boy."

"No, that's *my* boy," Dixie murmured. "And that's absolutely incredible!" Her breath caught in her throat as she realized her gaze was locked on the ruggedly handsome man, and not on the horse she'd dreamed of for so long.

Erik ran his hands up and down Victory's head and neck until the animal was completely quiet beneath his gentle touch. Watching his hands gently caressing the horse's quivering muscles, her skin began to tingle.

Then, taking his time, and with more patience than Dixie's wildly pumping heart could imagine, Erik picked up a bristle brush and followed the same path his hands had taken earlier, finishing by grooming his tail and calmly picking up each leg to examine the hooves.

He spoke in a low monotone the entire time, telling Victory what a fine-looking horse he was and how well he was doing today. It brought tears to

Dixie's eyes just to watch, and her heart was brimming with emotions she was afraid to identify.

"That was the hard part, my fine boy," Erik explained to the horse in the same low monotone. "The rest is like stealing sugar from my pocket."

He removed the long lead from the halter and replaced it with a short one, looping it around Victory's neck.

Dixie held her breath. Erik was going to attempt to ride the horse. She felt a jolt of jealousy, but stilled it as she watched in amazement.

Still speaking nonstop, Erik slid easily onto the horse's bare back, with so little fuss Dixie doubted Victory even knew Erik's intentions at all. Then Erik clicked his tongue, and the two were off.

Victory didn't buck and protest as Dixie would have expected. Instead, horse and man moved at an easy pace around the corral. No objection, not even a whinny, as Erik put the horse through his paces.

It was amazing. Incredible.

And she was green with envy.

Jealous of the horse, as much as of the man.

There was something in the way Erik looked at Victory and spoke to him that made her heart turn over. She wondered what it would be like to have Erik look at her that special, loving way, speak those soft, affectionate tones into her ears.

But she shook the thought away, replacing it with

the opposite side of the coin. Erik had a nasty habit of interceding on her behalf, taking care of her.

Well, she didn't want to be taken care of by a man. Especially this generous, attractive man whose very presence pulled on her heartstrings.

She was fine on her own. She had to be. And *she* wanted to be the one bonding with Victory, riding with the wind blowing in her hair.

The mountain air pinched her lungs as she struggled with her emotions. This was obviously Erik's God-given gift, training horses. But in fulfilling his special gift, he'd taken away hers.

It was high time to make her presence known.

Chapter Eleven

❧

Victory was a beauty, all right, Erik thought. He was going to be a great trail horse when he was properly trained, and Erik had enough confidence in his own abilities to know it wouldn't take long.

He could easily picture Dixie riding this fine mount, her satin-black hair brushed back in the wind, exposing her peaches-and-cream complexion to the bright sunshine. Her eyes would shine with her usual cheerfulness, combined with her passion for life.

Victory broke into a canter that matched the rhythm of Erik's heartbeat. He wanted to see Dixie on this horse. He wanted to be the one to put her there.

He swallowed hard and urged the horse into a gallop.

Vic had an excellent, comfortable gait, and he was a smart young horse. Erik knew it with the same gut instinct that told him the horse was ready for Dixie to ride, with his assistance.

He couldn't wait to share the news with Dixie, let her know her new horse had the makings of a fine trail horse. Put her up in front of him, wrap his arms around her and show her firsthand the thrill of the wind in her face as they galloped together through the open fields.

"What are you doing with Victory?"

Startled, Erik pulled back on the reins too hard and Victory protested, bucking beneath him.

How long had she been here? He'd been certain he was alone. He'd been so wrapped up in the horse, in surprising Dixie, that he hadn't detected her presence.

And he sure never expected to see her again this soon. He figured she'd be wallowing in self-pity for at least a day.

He should have known better.

He sure did now. Far from self-pity, she was angry again, though she looked more beautiful than ever with her aqua eyes blazing and her arms akimbo.

He wet his dry bottom lip with the tip of his tongue. "Just trying him out."

"No, you weren't."

"What?" He slid off the horse and led him to where Dixie stood, near the edge of the corral.

"No, you weren't," she repeated. "You weren't *trying Victory out*. I don't know exactly what you *were* doing, but some things are obvious enough. Do you care to explain?"

She sounded angry, but the harshness was tempered with curiosity.

He shrugged. It was obviously a rhetorical question. His attention was better spent on his horse.

Her horse.

She wasn't really interested in what he'd been doing with Victory, putting him through his paces so Dixie could ride him.

Her only concern was that he'd done it without her permission. Just like the stubborn woman. The fluttery feeling in his chest settled into lead in his gut.

"Well?" she demanded, and then softer, "I'd really like to know."

Surprised, he met her gaze and realized she was telling the truth. What he'd mistaken for anger was something else. Jealousy? At what?

Uncomfortable with emotions he couldn't identify in her, he cleared his throat. "Would you like to ride him?"

"Victory?" She sounded startled, almost alarmed.

He grinned. "He's your horse, isn't he?"

"Well, yes, but—"

"Then ride him."

Her eyes gleamed with excitement as her gaze turned to rest on Victory. "Oh. Okay."

She sounded a little shaky, but equally determined in her efforts.

He didn't blame her, after what had happened this afternoon. It was one of the reasons he'd taken Victory back to the corral in the first place. That and wanting to make Dixie smile, do something for her no one else around here could do.

Use his gift for horses to give her a gift.

Only, she wasn't supposed to find out about it.

He shook his head. Doing something nice for someone just because he—well, *liked* them, was a new experience for him. Uncomfortable. It threw him off center, like swinging around in circles on a Brahma bull.

She slid between the corral posts and walked up to Victory, holding out a sugar cube on her open palm. Despite her inexperience with horses, she looked as if she belonged there, with this horse.

Love flowed from her eyes, and Erik swallowed hard as he watched her.

"Hello, boy. Remember me?" she asked softly.

Her voice had a husky quality about it that turned Erik's knees to jelly.

He clenched his fists, needing to get a grip on it before he went and fell in love with her, or something equally foolish. Like maybe diving off the side of a cliff headfirst without looking to see where he would land.

He knew firsthand what love did to a man. His father wasted away when his mother died in childbirth with her third baby. Erik had only been eight, but he knew it was love that made his father go away.

Andrew Wheeler had become a shell of a man, working himself to death, unable to share his love with the children who reminded him so very much of her.

How could God do this to a man, never mind the small boys who'd grown up virtually without parents?

It was a battle his father fought until his grave.

And Erik still fought it now. As a man, Erik understood his father's pain, but as a child, all he'd known was that empty ache, the feeling of rejection he could never quite shake off.

And his brothers hadn't fared much better.

Rhett's wife left him, and Ethan hid under the security of his expensive business suits and mounds of money.

Erik shook his head, not allowing his thoughts to go further. Loving a woman made a man weak. Period.

And God made him weaker. He wouldn't let it

happen to him, no matter how his heart leapt like a calf whenever Dixie was around.

He was a man. Of course he reacted to seeing a beautiful woman. What man wouldn't?

He might not be able to control his longings, nor even his stray thoughts when he got a whiff of her perfume or when she faced him off with her stunning eyes shooting sparks.

But he could—would—control his actions.

Firming his jaw, he walked Victory around in a small circle, wrestling within himself to turn his attention to the horse and not the woman. He had faith that Victory was ready to ride, but Dixie would need him here to help work out the kinks.

"Ready?" he asked gruffly.

She nodded, her eyes wide. The color of the ocean, he thought distractedly.

He jerked his shoulders as he warded off the thought. The horse snorted and yanked his head on the lead, and Erik chided himself for getting sidetracked again, and so easily.

See? He was already showing weakness. And if there was one thing he despised, it was a weak man.

"The hardest part is going to be mounting. He's still a little skittish when he can't see what's going on. Just slide on him nice and easy."

Erik talked to Dixie, but made eye contact with Victory, calming the horse with his gaze.

Get 2

HOW TO GET YOUR
2 FREE BOOKS AND FREE GIFT

1. Peel off the 2 FREE BOOKS seal from the front cover. Place it in the space provided at right. This automatically entitles you to receive two free books and an exciting mystery gift.

2. Send back this card and you'll get 2 Love Inspired® novels. These books have a combined cover price of $9.00 in the U.S. and $10.50 in Canada, but they are yours to keep absolutely FREE!

3. There's <u>no</u> catch. You're under <u>no</u> obligation to buy anything. We charge nothing – ZERO – for your first shipment. And you don't have to make any minimum number of purchases – not even one!

4. We call this line Love Inspired because each month you'll receive novels that are filled with joy, faith and true Christian values. The stories will lift your spirits and gladden your heart! You'll like the convenience of getting them delivered to your home well before they are in stores. And you'll like our discount prices too!

5. We hope that after receiving your free books you'll want to remain a subscriber. But the choice is yours – to continue or cancel, anytime at all! So why not take us up on our invitation, with no risk of any kind. You'll be glad you did!

6. And remember…we'll send you a mystery gift ABSOLUTELY FREE just for giving Love Inspired   a try!

Steeple
Hill®

SPECIAL FREE GIFT!

We'll send you a fabulous mystery gift, absolutely FREE, simply for accepting our no-risk offer!

©1997 STEEPLE HILL

Dixie eyed the large Appaloosa, then began to walk hesitantly around him.

"Place a hand on his rear to let him know you're there. Otherwise, you're liable to get kicked," Erik instructed. "Come on over here to the left of the horse, and I'll boost you up."

She looked relieved. He'd been mounting horses since he was knee-high to a grasshopper, but Dixie was obviously new to this, and she was a great deal shorter than he was. He chuckled.

He was unused to laughing, yet it happened often when he was around Dixie. The smell of fresh peaches alone could make him smile.

He wouldn't follow that thought to its natural conclusion. Or any conclusion at all.

One thing he knew for sure—he couldn't touch her. He cupped his hands to offer her a lift, but she just stared at his laced fingers, perplexed. "What's wrong? Put your boot on my hands and climb aboard."

She wrinkled her nose. "But my boot's filthy," she protested.

He laughed from his belly this time. "It's okay. Really. I don't mind."

She raised her eyebrows. "That is the most disgusting thing I've ever heard of in my life."

He grunted and leaned against the horse's neck.

"Can't you lift me up?" she asked peevishly.

"That's what I was trying to do," he snapped

back, more annoyed with his own reaction to her than with her words.

"Erik," she warned, letting him know she didn't buy his sudden thickheadedness. She held her arms toward him, gesturing for him to pick her up.

His lungs burned as he struggled to inhale. Didn't the stubborn woman realize what she was asking of him?

No. Of course not. Why would she? To her, he was nothing more than her foreman. And right now she was expecting him to do his job.

He exhaled what air was left in his lungs, concentrating on the burning tightness in his chest. She wasn't giving him any choice. He thought he might choke. Strangle.

Reluctantly he stepped forward, reaching for her waist. The scent of peaches nearly drove him mad. His large, rough hands easily spanned her waist. She was so tiny, so vulnerable.

He wanted to kiss her. And suddenly he knew he would kiss her.

She lifted her hands to his shoulders and tilted her chin up toward his, inadvertently encouraging him.

Victory wandered to the edge of the corral, intent on the long grass peeking through the railing, but Dixie didn't appear to notice. Her gaze was caught with Erik's.

He hesitated, his head swimming with the scent

of peaches. He should go retrieve Victory, but his feet felt glued to the ground.

It would take little more than the slightest shift for their lips to meet, and he knew the moment when she realized it, too, the moment she tensed in his arms and tried to pull away.

But it was already too late. Too late to back out. He could no more not kiss her than stop his own heart from pounding in his ears.

He bent toward her, closing his eyes, soaking up the experience with his other dynamically amplified senses. Framing her face, he brushed his lips softly over hers, the merest butterfly kiss, yet a world-rocking revelation.

The skin on her face was every bit as soft and smooth as he'd imagined it to be, a marked contrast to his rough, callused fingertips. Her warm breath, coming in short bursts, met and mixed with his.

When she sighed and leaned into him, he kissed her again, deeper this time, wanting her to experience with him the myriad of feelings that swirled around and through him like the colors of a rainbow.

"No." He heard Dixie's voice, almost a whimper, from somewhere beyond the haze he was feeling. His equilibrium had disappeared, leaving him feeling as if he were floating upside down, but her single word cut through to the center of his soul.

Immediately he dropped his hands from her and stepped back, uncomfortable with the way she stared at him, her eyes wide with a mixture of wonder and apprehension.

She opened her mouth, then snapped it closed. Apparently she was as stunned by his actions as he was.

As his world righted, his conscience pricked him, and he wondered if he should apologize. He wondered if he could.

I know. I shouldn't have kissed you.

But he found himself unable to say the words out loud, so he just shrugged.

"Don't do that again." She scowled, her voice low and raspy.

He felt a moment of panic when she spoke, wondering if he'd ruined everything, if she might fire him for his presumption.

But a moment later, his panic abated as she walked over to the grazing horse and grasped his uneven mane in one hand, lifting her foot to be boosted up onto his back.

Her gaze was clear, as if nothing had happened between them. Maybe that's the way she wanted it to be.

Maybe it was for the best.

He strode to her side and cupped his hands, helping her mount. Victory shifted, but didn't protest. He probably barely felt petite Dixie on his back.

Erik handed her one end of the rope, keeping the other to lead her around the corral.

"Comfortable?" he asked. If she was going to ignore the sparks between them, he could do no less. Or more.

She sat ramrod-straight and stiff as a mannequin. "This is the first time I've ever ridden bareback," she admitted in a wobbly voice.

And probably the second time she'd ever ridden in her life, Erik added silently. "It's better to learn to ride this way first. Close your eyes."

"What?" she exclaimed, causing Victory to side-step. Then whispering, she continued. "You're kidding, right? Close my eyes?"

What? Did she think he was going to try to kiss her again?

"I've got the horse in hand, Dixie," he pointed out wryly. "Close your eyes and feel him shift. It'll help your other senses become attuned to the way Victory moves beneath you."

He ran a hand down Victory's neck, then scratched him behind the ears, eliciting a low whicker in response. "The goal of a good rider is to become one with the horse. You have to learn the peculiarities unique to Victory. Then he'll never surprise you." He struggled to keep a straight face. "Most of the time, anyway."

Looking chagrined, Dixie closed her eyes.

He smiled, knowing she couldn't see him. There was something oddly wonderful about teasing her.

"I can feel it," she said, her voice low in awe.

"I can feel it, Erik. His muscles, his stride. This is glorious."

Erik swallowed around the lump in his throat. "Good," he said gruffly. "Now open your eyes, but keep your concentration focused on the horse."

She did as she was told, her face radiant with this new discovery.

"And try to relax. You won't ever blend with the horse if you don't loosen your posture. You look like a brick wall up there."

"Oh," she said, her brow furrowing as she concentrated. "There. Is that better?"

He nodded. "Want to try a trot?"

"Do you think I can?"

"I think you can do anything you put your mind to," he replied, enormously aware of his double meaning.

They spent another hour together in the ring. Dixie was a natural horsewoman, someone who automatically did things right without having to be told. And when he did have to instruct her, it only took once.

He showed her how to hold the reins, how to direct Victory to the right and to the left, and the most important command, *whoa.*

She absorbed everything, her expression as bright as the morning star. He'd never seen anyone who took such joy in living, or who worked so hard to get things right.

As she slid down from the horse, he grasped her hips for support, marveling that his hands spanned the entire width of her waist. She was so tiny, yet so strong on the inside. He'd never met a woman like her.

"I can't believe I'm riding him already," she said excitedly.

"We'll put a bridle on him tomorrow and see how he does."

She whipped around, surprised. "You're not obligated to help me out with Victory. I know you're really busy with the stable and all. I appreciate what you've already done, Erik, but taking care of my personal concerns isn't part of your contract."

He stiffened. Was she trying to tell him she didn't want his help? Or was she afraid of being kissed again? He wasn't all that certain he could keep from kissing her.

But she was being stubborn.

And it wasn't the first time. Couldn't the woman see he was doing her a favor?

"I won't…" he began, then broke off, determined to start over. "You're going to need help," he ground out, feeling obligated to state the obvious, and ignoring the rest.

Erik's words were like sandpaper to Dixie, who immediately bristled against the pressure. She didn't want to depend on anyone, least of all this strong, silent cowboy who kept coming to her rescue. When

Erik kissed her, fireworks exploded within her. And it scared her to death. She'd never before experienced anything remotely close to what she felt in Erik's arms—not even with Abel.

Was this the way it was supposed to be between a man and a woman?

No. Not between her and Erik.

Why couldn't he just leave her and her horse alone?

She glared at him for a full minute, then blew out a breath and looked away. "You're right, of course."

He had no idea how painful it was to admit she needed his help. Especially now, when everything had changed between them, whether Erik knew it or not. But she didn't even know how to ride well, never mind how to train a green broke yearling.

And despite her relative ignorance where horses were concerned, she was certain the progress Erik had made with Victory this afternoon went above and beyond usual expectations. She certainly hadn't expected to be able to ride him so soon.

Her lack of knowledge plagued her. She wasn't even sure she could bridle him, though she'd paid careful attention in her reading to that very thing, had even drawn pictures to illustrate the practice.

But if there was one thing she'd learned from her time in South Dakota, it was that all the reading and education in the world didn't help much when confronted by the real McCoy, which happened every time she turned around, up to and including Victory, the green broke gelding.

She had a double major in missions and outdoor recreation, and it hadn't helped her one bit so far. She couldn't even put up her own tent, never mind pick a horse she could ride. And while she didn't regret her heartfelt purchase, she knew Victory was more than she could presently handle on her own.

It galled her, but she needed Erik.

"I don't mind," he said, his voice gruff. "We can meet here every afternoon for an hour, if you want." He reached for a bristle brush and began grooming Victory.

"Am I really going to be able to ride him?" she asked softly, holding her breath in anticipation of his answer, knowing he would tell her the truth even if it wasn't what she wanted to hear.

He glanced up, then returned his gaze to his work. "Yep."

She was silent for a moment, observing the man with the horse, marveling at how gifted he was. She laid a hand on his forearm, stopping the motion of the brush. The touch was like a live wire of electricity between them. He stared at her hand on his arm, his jaw tensing.

"Erik?" she scratched out when she could speak.

"Hmm?"

"Thanks for helping me learn to ride."

She whirled on the toes of her boots and marched back toward the main lodge, escaping, thinking to go anywhere but where Erik was.

She knew him well enough to know he didn't like to be thanked for anything, proud man that he was.

Her heart clenched. It hurt too much to see him turn away from her again. And that's exactly what she knew he would do, if given the opportunity. Just like Abel, and everyone else in her life. She ran people off like a virus.

It didn't take a rocket scientist to tell her she made him nervous, especially when she said things he didn't want to hear. Like how special he was, and how blessed she was to have him working for her.

How God was moving in her life. And how He would work in Erik's life, as well. She prayed every day God would soften Erik's hard heart and take away his resentment and anger, as only God could.

She knew he suffered from some deep internal wounds, but of course he wouldn't talk about it. God would have to change his heart, for Dixie failed at every attempt.

As the days went by, her prayers were becoming more intense. It was certainly a life-or-death matter, and not only for Erik. Dixie's heart was dangling from his sleeve, and that was a very dangerous place to be.

Chapter Twelve

Erik groomed and fed Vic and placed him in his stall, fighting off his thoughts as he did his work. But he could only ignore his nagging mind for so long. He had to get away from this place before he shattered like a fist through glass.

He saddled a black mare named Jazz and headed for the hills, toward the stream that ran through the acreage. Maybe in the quiet of the mountains, he'd find his peace. And maybe, just maybe, answer the interminable question nagging him.

What was he going to do about Dixie?

He couldn't let things go on the way they were, yet he hadn't the slightest idea how to change circumstances so they would work out.

In truth, he didn't really know *what* he wanted, only that he was miserable.

He was attracted to Dixie. Why hadn't he seen that before, he wondered, finding a cool spot by the stream to tether his horse. The insight didn't come easily or willingly. He'd give anything *not* to feel anything for the crazy, stubborn woman.

But he was too analytical to ignore the facts. And the facts pointed to one thing—he was falling head over snakeskin boots in love with Dixie Sullivan.

No matter how he swore off women, or how often the imp on his shoulder reminded him of the dangers loving a woman presented, it had happened. Despite his convictions, despite his resolve.

Was God in this somewhere?

The question badgered him persistently for the next half hour as he sat along the bank of the stream and tossed gravel into the water. A man couldn't truly love Dixie without God playing into the picture somewhere.

Her faith could move mountains. God was the center of her life. How often had he seen her resting in the shade of a tree, reading her worn and tattered Bible?

She talked about God like He was some kind of personal friend or something, not this monstrous, omniscient entity a million miles away in heaven as Erik imagined Him to be.

He moved his hand to cover the pocket of his Western shirt, reaching for the reassurance of the small, rectangular object lodged between the fabric and his skin.

Dixie had presented him with the small New Testament and Psalms the first day he worked for her. He knew he hadn't been singled out, that it hadn't been a gift just for him, but then again, if it were, would he have accepted it?

Probably not. And probably Dixie would have known that.

As it was, she gave the same small, maroon leather Bible to each and every one of her staff. He kept his copy on him wherever he went, tucked away in his pocket, next to his heart.

He coughed as his throat tightened around his breath. He was going lame in the head. His brothers would tease him to no end about this suddenly sentimental, romantic tendency of his.

He'd never actually cracked the book and read it, though he knew Dixie hoped he would. She called the Bible *God's Word,* and spoke of it as if it was truly a letter from God to man.

He didn't want to admit it, but the Bible intimidated him. Who was *he* to read a book written by God through His prophets? Erik wasn't even a believer.

He ought to toss it in the trash and be done with it, yet he couldn't.

Crazy, was what it was. Insane.

But it felt somehow right to keep the Bible in his

pocket, a part of Dixie to carry around with him while he did his work.

Now, in the quiet of the meadow with nothing but the gurgle of the stream as background music, he pulled the small maroon book from his pocket and held it in his palm, reflecting on its light weight compared to the heaviness in his heart.

How did a man read the Bible, anyway?

Just open up to page one and dive in? Or was there some secret formula Christians used to know where to read? He knew the chapters and verses were marked with numbers.

Where was he supposed to start?

Dixie would know, but he wasn't about to ask her. Just like she'd know how to talk to God. But maybe you had to be one of God's special friends to have that privilege. Erik certainly hadn't earned that.

He pulled in a deep breath and blew it out again in a rush. "Okay, Lord. If You're there, You're gonna need to help me."

He rifled through the pages, then turned to *Matthew 1:1* and started reading. He wasn't a fast reader, but he had nowhere to be and no one expecting him, so he didn't feel rushed.

He read of Jesus's birth, how as a boy He remained in the temple with His parents frantic to find Him, how He grew in stature and wisdom with both God and man.

He got as far as the devil tempting Jesus before

it really began to sink in. Jesus hadn't eaten in forty days. He must have been weak, famished. Yet when Satan reminded Jesus of His ability to make bread from stones, His answer struck Erik right between the eyes.

Man shall not live by bread alone, but by every word that proceeds from the mouth of God.

Was that why Dixie insisted on giving each staff member a Bible? Because she knew they weren't living a full life without God?

Lightning quick, he snapped his own little New Testament shut and tucked it back in his pocket, almost as if it were hot to the touch.

He'd never needed God's Word before. Why should he need it now?

But he couldn't stop thinking of the passage, thinking about the gap in his life. Food, water, clothing—who better than Erik knew it wasn't enough, no matter how he fooled himself? Deep in his heart, he knew even his own herd of horses wouldn't make him feel complete.

He needed love.

Was that why he was so drawn to Dixie? Because she offered not only the love of a beautiful woman, but the love of God?

He grabbed the largest rock in his reach and threw it with all his might, missing the river and making a cloud of dust on the opposite bank. Anger and pain roiled through the empty places in his heart.

What right did he have to ask for God's love? It wasn't only that he hadn't believed, for deep in his heart he'd always known there was a God. The creation of the horse alone was too exquisite to have been mere chance.

But he'd turned from that God, thrown blame on that God. Hated Him for taking away his mother, and by that, his father.

How could God forgive him?

It was too wide a gap to bridge, even for Dixie's all-loving God.

And Dixie?

Dixie thought of him as the big lug of a cowboy who more often got in her way as not. How many times did she remind him not to run things for her, or accuse him of trying to overprotect her?

How many times had he seen anger sparkling in those pools of aqua-blue?

As if that weren't enough, there was Abel to contend with. Her ex-fiancé, the near-perfect missionary man strong enough to give up Dixie's love to do God's will.

Abel, a man nearly elevated to sainthood, at least in Dixie's eyes. Even though he'd left her in the lurch.

Abel, who never thought of himself, but only the God he served and the people under his care.

Abel, who had won Dixie's heart with his kind ways and fancy words.

Erik didn't want to think about Abel, but he couldn't help but compare. He realized the emotion he'd been feeling when she spoke of another man, a man who'd broken her heart and left no room for another.

Jealousy.

Pure, unadulterated jealousy.

It didn't make a bit of difference in the long run, except to make him more miserable than he already was.

Erik knew he wasn't ever going to be the right man for Dixie Sullivan, not if he worked at it until he was a thousand years old.

She needed a man with a strong faith in God. A man who didn't bring with him the baggage of a miserable past. A man who could love Dixie the way she deserved to be loved.

A man like Abel Kincaid.

Besides, Erik thought, she didn't even like him.

Tolerated him, perhaps. Maybe even considered him a friend, given the amount of time they spent with each other.

His throat continued to strangle him. He didn't want friendship. Not anymore.

But when he tried to move forward, make their relationship more, she'd backed off. What was a cowboy to do?

He already knew the consequences of this self-examination, this discovery—maybe more an admission than a discovery—of his feelings for Dixie.

If he'd been tongue-tied around her before, he knew it was going to be at least doubly as bad now. Every time she looked at him with anger or hurt in her eyes, the pain was going to pierce his chest twice as hard.

The smell of peaches was going to have him fainting like a little old lady.

He mounted Jazz and galloped through the meadow, hoping the wind would take the edge off the pain searing his heart.

There was nothing he could do about his love for Dixie, except be there when she needed him, and protect her from those who would hurt her, as Ellis had done. He would be her right-hand man even when she insisted she didn't need one.

It was the least he could do. And the most.

Chapter Thirteen

She could ride! She could really ride!

In the month since Erik had begun teaching her to ride on Victory, she'd learned to saddle and bridle the horse, taking care to tighten the cinch against Victory's stubborn inclination to bloat when she saddled him.

She'd learned how to groom him, feed him a more substantial fare than sugar cubes and clean the mud from his hooves with a pick. She'd learned to mount and dismount without Erik's assistance.

And she'd learned to ride.

Okay, so she wasn't galloping through the fields yet. But Erik often complimented her on her natural seat and instinctive use of her body and knees in guiding the horse.

She could walk, trot and even canter, although she

still felt like grasping the saddle horn when Victory got going at such a fast clip. She didn't dare make that amateur mistake, not after the first time Erik chewed her out for it.

He wouldn't let her take her free hand from her thigh, telling her if she was going to learn to ride, she'd learn to ride right. She was afraid of the consequences if she didn't. He threatened to hold the hand there himself.

Just the thought made her skin tingle.

She needed to learn to *feel* the horse, move *with* the horse instead of fighting him. Not think about Erik.

There would be no need for a saddle horn when she learned to be one with the horse, he assured her. She wasn't sure at this point if she'd get past the bumbling part, not as long as she had a handsome cowboy as a teacher.

She smiled softly, hearing his gentle instruction even now.

Grip with your knees. Lean backward going downhill, forward going uphill. Relax. Relax. Relax.

With the horse, at least, she was starting to relax, starting to feel her dream broaching reality. Erik Wheeler was another matter entirely. The more time she spent with him, the harder it became to concentrate—at least on learning to ride. Yet, ironically, Erik was the means to the fulfillment of a lifelong dream. *Many* lifelong dreams, some only recently coming to light.

Or maybe it wasn't quite as ironic as it first appeared.

She shook her thoughts from her mind. She had work to do, and here she was, daydreaming again.

She found it infinitely more pleasurable to think about her horse—and about the man who trained him—than to consider the overwhelming number of tasks left to do before the members of her church arrived in two weeks.

The buildings were complete, and the retreat itself looked wonderful. Riding and hiking trails were well established.

She'd been working to build respect with the stable hands. Tally had taken over as the unofficial leader of the hands. She had high hopes the other boys would follow his example and stop harassing her. She'd been working alongside them, deciding actions would speak louder than words to the young men.

Today she'd rounded the hands together to make a final tour of the fencing around her land. It needed to be done, but she didn't necessarily have to be there. She wanted to be there.

Armed with a hammer and nails, she mounted Victory and took the lead as Tally and the others followed her to the outskirts of her land. The outside fence was made with split pine logs from her land.

It had only been a few weeks, but already, a little wear and tear was visible.

Mostly, it was just a pleasant ride. At least until they came to the gate leading to the Needleson property, which Dixie quickly assessed with her newly learned carpentry knowledge. The gate was twisted sideways off its hinges, looking very much as if it had been run over with a motor vehicle of some kind.

Sighing, Dixie dismounted and hobbled her horse, gesturing for the boys to do likewise. Planting her hands on her hips, she groaned. "Any of you boys know how to fix a mangled gate?"

Silence. She glanced around. The hands were staring back at her with dazed looks in their eyes.

"No carpenters in this bunch?" she asked, punctuating her sentence with a laugh.

Bushman, one of the younger hands, laughed low and deep. "We do horses, not hammers."

"Yeah," Hogan, the largest and eldest of the hands, piped in. "And this one looks like it definitely needs a hammer."

Dixie mock-frowned. "I thought ranch hands mended fences."

Tally made a face. "The unfun part of ranching."

Dixie smothered a grin. "You fellows would rather be horsin' around?"

The young men laughed in surprised unison.

"Plenty of time for that. First, we have a fence

to mend." She rummaged through her saddle pack for a hammer and nails.

Bushman followed her lead, hobbling his horse and walking to her side. "You're going to help?" he asked, astonishment lining his voice.

"Yes. And why wouldn't I?"

Hogan snickered, a sound that eternally ruffled Dixie's feathers. She tensed her shoulders, then relaxed. "Is there a reason that is funny?"

"No, ma'am," Tally interceded before Hogan could reply. "It's just that you—well, you're a city girl with enough money to buy a nice spread of land out of pocket. It seems…" His sentence drifted off for a moment as he struggled to choose the right word. "Weird. For you to get your hands dirty. I mean, why should you?"

She bristled. There was a little bit of resentment behind Tally's tone, Dixie realized, but then again, it was understandable. She'd put any misapprehensions to rest.

Right here. Right now.

"Oh, I see. City princess with loads of cash who has never seen a day's work in her life, never mind a lick of trouble, waltzes on this land and orders a passel of poor men around. Is that it?" She reined in her temper, but the backlash of her own resentment filled her voice nonetheless.

"Something like that," Hogan muttered under his breath.

She wanted to box his ears—or at least plant her fists on her hips while she argued with him, but instead she offered a silent prayer for patience and divine assistance with her words and actions.

This was the opportunity she'd been waiting for. The chance to really get to know these boys—make friends. If she lost her temper, she'd lose what God had graciously given her.

She walked toward the gate and tried to move it. It didn't budge. She put a shoulder to the wood and pushed, grunting with effort, to no avail.

Both her body and voice strained against the firm wood. "What's this gate made of, anyway? Lead?"

"It's not that," Tally answered, pointing at the juncture of the gate and the fence. "It's wedged into the post."

"Great," she muttered under her breath. She wiped a hand across her sweaty brow and continued. "Give me a hand, here."

The three young men gathered around the gate and, under Dixie's guidance, attempted to pull it up and out of the solid wood post.

"We need leverage," Dixie inserted, narrowing her eyes and looking around, her mind tossing about for an answer.

"Over there. Get a couple of those logs."

Tally lifted his eyebrows, then complied, Bushman taking the second log.

"Put the fat one on the ground. We'll use the

other across it as a lever to raise the gate. Then you brutes can pull it out.''

''Who is going to hold the lever?'' Hogan asked, taking his place at the side of the broken gate.

''Me.''

The young men chuckled, though none of them outright laughed.

She smiled cattily, then sat down on the *up* side of the teeter-totter log. She had to bounce once or twice, but slowly the gate moved up until it was parallel to the ground.

''Good going,'' Tally said, and the others nodded.

Dixie beamed with their grudging praise. ''Still think I'm a no-good city girl?''

''No, ma'am,'' Hogan answered, sounding just a little bit ashamed.

She probably had at least a dozen splinters on her backside, she thought, wincing. But it was worth it if she could get even one of these boys to see past the obvious, into the heart of things.

About her. And ultimately, about God. She couldn't very well show them God's love if they didn't respect her.

''I grew up different from you fellows,'' she continued, ''But not necessarily better.''

Hogan humphed, and Tally pinned him with a warning glare.

Dixie just smiled. ''Where do you think I got the money for this retreat?''

"Your papa," Bushman answered promptly.

It was Dixie's turn to snort. "Believe me, the last place my *papa* wants me to be is working in Christian ministry."

Even Tally looked surprised.

"I had to work and pray my way here. I traveled for two years from church to church, asking for support. It didn't come easy, partly because I'm a woman. I had to fight for my vision."

She looked from face to face, meeting each man's gaze. "I didn't give up. Sometimes all I could do was keep my eyes on the Lord. But I didn't quit."

"But you've known God for a long time," Bushman protested.

She shook her head. "I didn't grow up in the faith. I didn't even hear about God until I was seventeen. That's part of the reason I wanted to build this retreat. I want the little ones to hear about Jesus." She paused and waved a hand. "Pull just a hair to the left. I think we've almost got it."

"I never heard about God 'til here. Um, I mean now," Hogan admitted, his voice low and scratchy.

Dixie's throat caught, and tears sprang to her eyes, though she held them at bay by pinching her bottom lip between her teeth.

"It took me three more years to finally understand Jesus could love me. Bad childhood, wretched teen years and all."

"You did bad things?" Tally asked, sounding genuinely amazed.

Dixie nearly howled with laughter. "I must really look like Miss Goody Two-shoes to you fellows."

A low laugh came from behind her, sending Dixie's heart into her throat. She didn't hear Erik laugh often. She hadn't even known he was there, or she would have tried harder, she thought crossly.

She leaned back and tipped her head in order to see Erik. At the same time, the stable hands yanked on the gate, which gave suddenly without a sound, other than the muttered exclamations of the young men.

Dixie careened onto the ground with a bone-jarring bump, pounding the breath from her lungs as she landed flat on her back. She pinched her eyes closed, not wanting to see Erik's expression.

"You okay?"

She cracked one eye open.

Erik rested one forearm on the saddle horn of his mount and leaned over her, his mouth twitching at one corner.

If he laughed, Dixie thought she might scream. That is, if she had any breath left in her lungs, which she sincerely doubted.

"Playing teeter-totter?" Erik asked, grinning fully.

"Very funny," she groaned, surprised the young men didn't laugh with Erik.

"It was her idea to hoist this thing with these beams," Tally said, sounding defensive.

"Yeah," Hogan agreed. "These hinges are shot. But now that we've got the gate down, we'll have it fixed in a jiffy, boss."

Dixie raised her head. Hogan was looking at her.

"What happened?" Erik asked in his usual clipped tone.

"Looks like a truck ran this through," Bushman offered.

Erik scowled. "Needleson."

Dixie shook her head. "You don't know that."

Erik nudged his horse with his heels and began moving away without comment.

Annoyed, Dixie scrambled up as fast as her aching limbs would allow and reached for Victory. "Can you boys finish up here?"

"Yes, ma'am," they said in unison.

She nodded and mounted, turning Victory in the direction Erik had gone.

"You don't know it was Needleson," she called after him.

He turned his horse so abruptly she nearly ran Victory right up his nose.

"Needleson sold you a bum horse and you know it," he snapped.

"Victory is *not* a bum horse," she protested automatically, grinding her teeth against a further outburst. But despite her denial, doubt crept into her mind. Could John Needleson have sold her Victory as some sort of nasty prank? And who *had* run through the gate?

Needleson was the obvious culprit.

Her gazed locked with Erik's. He pinched his lips together, then shook his head. "I'll take care of it."

"You most certainly will not." Dixie maneuvered Victory until she was practically nose to nose with Erik. She could feel his warm breath on her face. Aqua eyes met and melded with the color of steel, and her heart felt just as cold.

"It could be John," she conceded reluctantly. "But until we have proof, I don't want to make trouble."

"Seems to me Needleson's the one making trouble." Erik leaned toward her, closing the distance between them.

"But I won't bother him," he said huskily. "For now. Still, if I find out he's trying to hurt you—"

He let the end of his sentence dangle in the air as he nudged his horse into a canter. In moments, he was out of Dixie's sight. But not out of mind, she thought, still trying to catch her breath.

Definitely not out of mind.

Erik couldn't ride fast enough or far enough. He hadn't known what to say when Dixie ordered him not to see John Needleson. He wasn't a *take-orders* kind of guy, especially where potential trouble was concerned.

And John Needleson was potential trouble. Erik recognized it just as surely as he'd recognized it in Ellis. And, as usual, he'd been stymied by Dixie's enduring faith in God and humankind. Her strength of character amazed him, her goodness and kindness daunted him.

Would he ever find the words to tell her how he felt?

Chapter Fourteen

A whole week later, Dixie was still mulling over her last encounter with Erik. She'd seen him two dozen times since, but he'd reverted to the silent, brooding cowboy she was used to.

The stable hands were beginning to trust her, if only a little. Now, if only she could convince Erik to follow their example. He was as aloof and silent as ever, and his actions—or lack of them, to be more precise—were driving her to the border of insanity.

She needed to talk about what was happening between them, if indeed anything was. She scolded herself for spending her valuable time and emotional resources thinking about the infuriating man.

She should be thinking about the people, her guests, who would soon descend on the retreat in droves. At least, she hoped they would. She'd booked a few church retreats beyond her own church's *grand opening* celebration, but the future was uncertain at best.

She needed to concentrate, but thoughts of Erik kept intruding, like a bothersome fly that buzzed around her head. No matter how many times she swatted him away, he just kept coming back for more.

She blew out a breath and surveyed her list. She had yet to receive the shipment of beds and basins for the individual cabins, though the main lodge was now furnished with everything from dining tables to appropriately rustic-looking curtains for the windows, and the staff cabins were likewise ornamented.

She still needed a truckload of linens, not to mention the food needed to feed fifty people, not including her staff, for two weeks.

She'd been putting off going to town, unwilling to miss out on her daily riding lesson. But it had to be done sometime, and today was as good a day as any, she decided spontaneously.

Checking to make sure she had the appropriate lists with her, she climbed into the cab of her truck and started the engine. It wasn't until she attempted to pull out that she realized something was wrong.

The truck wasn't moving properly, with the horsepower the all-terrain vehicle usually exhibited. In fact, it was barely moving at all.

Baffled, Dixie cut the engine and exited the cab, wondering if anyone on the premises knew anything about fixing cars. She was the last person on earth who could tell what was wrong with her truck, or at least she thought so, until she surveyed the outside of her truck.

She might not be able to tell a muffler from a radiator, but it didn't take a trained auto mechanic to see that her tires had been slashed.

All four of them.

That it was no accident was equally as evident, for the bowie knife used to perform the deed had been left in a conspicuous spot on the hood of the truck, holding down a folded piece of notebook paper like a paperweight.

If she hadn't been so preoccupied with other matters, she would have noticed it earlier.

Anger flared. Who would do this to her?

The stable boys, for a laugh.

Ellis, to get back at her for firing him.

Erik, just so he could come to her rescue again.

John Needleson.

That thought just added fuel to the fire. A grown man wouldn't play a nasty, immature trick like this, would he?

She snatched the gleaming, unsheathed bowie knife from the hood and opened the paper beneath.

"Go home. You don't belong here."

It wasn't signed.

"O-o-o-o-h!" she yelled, venting her anger aloud as she stomped back and forth, surveying the truck's damage. She screamed so loud, even James the cook popped his head out the kitchen window to see what the ruckus was about.

It didn't take long for Erik to appear at her side. He always seemed to be around to see her fall apart during a crisis, she thought resentfully.

Why should today be any different?

Not that he could help in this situation, unless he knew how to magically patch tires.

Horses, he knew. Cars, she doubted. He didn't look like the greasy, under-the-hood type.

She mentally calculated how much it would cost to get her truck towed on a flatbed into Custer, and cringed at the dollar amount.

A second job was beginning to look like a necessity. She'd considered the option since she'd arrived in South Dakota, but it still disturbed her to have her hand forced. It wasn't going to be easy.

She'd have to commute into the small town to waitress or something. Every moment working in town would be a moment away from directing her retreat. And she wouldn't have any more free time to ride Victory.

The thought didn't do anything to elevate her mood, which was quickly deflating to the level of her truck tires.

In typical Erik fashion, he didn't say a word, but

crouched down by the truck, examining the tires. Anger sparkled in his eyes, simmering just below the surface, carefully controlled with the strength of his will.

For some reason, that annoyed her. What did he have to be angry about? It was her truck tires that were slashed. He could go right back to the stable and forget all about it.

But he wouldn't. He'd step in and try to take over, like he always did.

And for another, why was he always so *in control?*

Once, just once, she'd like to see him overcome with anger—or any emotion, for that matter. She'd like to see him lose his cool. Really blow it, as she did on a regular basis.

"This was no accident," he said, his voice low and gravelly.

"No kidding," she snapped back. "Here's the knife that did the dirty deed." She dropped it at his feet.

"You touched it."

"Well, of course I touched it. There was a letter—" She stopped midsentence, realizing her error. Disturbing evidence at the scene of the crime.

Erik grunted in disgust. With her, most likely. "Where's the letter?"

"Should I call the police?" she asked, answering

a question with a question. When Erik didn't answer, she sighed and handed him the letter.

"No." It was almost a growl.

"No, what?"

He glanced up, his blue eyes so dark they were almost black under the rim of his Stetson. "You probably shouldn't call the police."

He was right. She had nothing to go on, and what little evidence she did have, she'd already tampered with, not that she thought a set of fingerprints would amount to much in a town as small as Custer.

The note was definitely a plus, but it wasn't signed, and she suspected handwriting analysts were few and far between this far out.

"Well, in any case, I do have to call a tow truck. And then I've got to deal with whatever spiteful vandal slashed my tires."

She shivered. "Do you think it's one of my staff? One of the stable boys, maybe? Or was it Ellis?"

He frowned. "I'll drive you to town. We can pick tires up there and I'll put them on myself. You can get them aligned later."

Pulling his hat off by the crown, he swiped his forearm against his temple. "Ellis wouldn't be stupid enough to pull a stunt like this."

Angry heat flared to her cheeks. Ellis was stupid enough to do a lot of other spiteful things, most of them right to her face.

Why not slash her tires?

"You don't think so?" she retorted, her voice higher, louder and squeakier than she would have liked.

His stone-cold gaze settled on her. "No. I don't. But I'll check it out while we're in town. If he did slash your tires, he's in for it."

Dixie shuddered. She didn't like violence, and she felt the rage barely contained within Erik. Suddenly the idea of him blowing his top wasn't as agreeable as it once had sounded.

And she still didn't know why it mattered to him.

What difference did it make whether or not Ellis slashed her tires? It wasn't all that long ago Erik himself wasn't so keen on her being here, though she liked to think she'd changed his opinion on that subject over time.

If someone was trying to run her off the land, he should be rejoicing, not commiserating.

John Needleson.

Her eyes met Erik's and his gaze confirmed her fear. He was thinking the same thing. And this time she wasn't sure he'd keep his promise to keep his hands off.

He strode to his truck and opened the passenger door, gesturing for her to hurry. He didn't have to speak for her to feel the tension in the air, tension between them, and tension aimed at the unknown vandal.

The drive to town in Erik's truck was made in

silence. Dixie was busy with her own thoughts, and Erik—well, he was being Erik. He didn't speak until they pulled up in front of the auto shop in Custer.

"If you can't get what you need here, we'll drive up to Rapid City," he said, leaning his forearms against the steering wheel. "I'll pick you up in about an hour. We'll know better, then."

Her eyes widened. He was leaving her here? What did she know about tires? Besides, she knew he was going to ask after Ellis.

And that was none of his business.

She opened her mouth to protest, then snapped it shut again. Hadn't she just been complaining that no one ever took her seriously, that Erik didn't believe she could do anything by herself?

And here she was about to whine about her lack of knowledge where truck tires were concerned.

Go figure.

Scowling, she got out of the truck and slammed the door. Hard.

She'd figure this out on her own if she had to go to the public library and read a book about buying truck tires.

She could swear Erik was chuckling as he turned out of the parking lot. A loud protest welled in her, but she held back, knowing the object of her wrath was on his way to investigate Ellis and wouldn't hear her even if she screamed down the road. Which she was mighty tempted to do, whether he could hear it or not.

She took several deep breaths and consciously unclenched her fists.

Let him laugh. She'd show him just what Dixie Sullivan could do if she put her mind to it.

She didn't need a man in her life to order her around and protect her when she didn't need protection.

Even Erik Wheeler.

Erik was loathe to leave her alone, even within the safety of town limits. Someone was being nasty. Very nasty. If he were a gambling man, he'd put his money on John Needleson.

But he'd promised Dixie to follow up with Ellis, and he intended to keep his word. If it didn't take him long, he might be able to ask a few pertinent questions around town. Starting with Mary in the post office. If there was any new gossip running around, Mary would know it.

He clamped his jaw until his teeth hurt, and reluctantly turned his truck down the lane toward Ellis's grandmother's house. His gut told him he was wasting his time. And time was working against him. He wouldn't let anyone harm Dixie, if that was the vandal's intent.

That's what Erik was determined to find out.

Chapter Fifteen

Dixie leaned against the metal frame of the garage door, watching a kid about the same age as her stable hands straining against a lug wrench. He was only on the second tire of the lady's car that was in front of Dixie, and it had been nearly an hour. Time certainly didn't mean the same thing in Custer as it did in Denver.

A ten-minute lube had obviously never been heard of in these parts. She thought it might be more efficient to take off all four tires and then replace them with the new ones, but she hesitated to suggest it. The kid was the expert, she supposed.

"Problems?" a dry, scratchy voice asked from beside her.

She turned to see John Needleson staring at her. He was smiling, but it was more of a gloating smile than a friendly smile. Suspicion flashed through her mind, and her shoulders tensed.

"Nothing that I can't handle."

"That so?"

She stared at him, and he stared back angrily. Suspicion turned to knowledge. He was out-and-out baiting her, perhaps attempting to rail her into accusing him of slashing her tires.

And she wanted to. Oh, how she wanted to tell him she knew everything. Demand the truth from him. What did he have against her?

But a still, small voice tapped her on the shoulder, and she froze, taking deep breaths to relieve the tension in her muscles. Anger wouldn't win any wars.

Only love could do that.

She didn't deserve God's grace. Could she do less for John? *Do unto others...*

There was pain behind John's angry gaze. There was a reason animosity shone from his eyes. She didn't know the whole story. It was enough to know his need was there. Dixie wanted to point him to the One who could help him deal with his wife's death.

"I'm glad to see you, John," she said softly, genuinely. "I want to get to know my neighbors better."

His breath caught in what sounded like a snort. "Don't need no *neighbors* intruding."

She was taken aback, as if slapped. "I didn't mean to intrude."

"Well, you are."

She wanted to point out that he'd been the one to approach her, but the point seemed moot. He didn't appear to be talking about here and now.

"Are you here in town for supplies?" she asked, trying a different tack.

He grunted in response.

Funny, that he should be at the garage at the exact time she'd come to get her slashed tires repaired. The hair stood up on the back of Dixie's neck.

"I love riding Victory." She didn't know whether she was searching for a compatible subject, or baiting him.

His bushy gray eyebrows rose high on his forehead. There was no missing his astonishment.

"I didn't know he was only green broke when I bought him."

His eyes narrowed. "You say you're riding him?"

She attempted a grimacing smile. "Absolutely."

He frowned. "Too bad."

He whirled on his heels and stomped away, muttering under his breath.

He'd sold her the colt on purpose.

Was he trying to harm her? What did he have to gain?

She strained to remember their short, one-sided conversation. What had he said about intruding neighbors? Is that how he felt about her?

Even grouchy neighbors didn't slash tires. John Needleson was definitely an enigma. One she meant to solve, with God's help.

And Erik's blissful ignorance of the entire situation. This was definitely, Dixie thought, one situation where what he *didn't* know wouldn't hurt him.

"It wasn't Ellis," Erik explained as they drove back to the retreat, four new truck tires tossed into the bed of his pickup.

His anger still simmered just below the surface, so he carefully tread on the words he spoke.

"How do you know?" snapped Dixie, pressing her fingers against her temples. "I'm getting a headache."

"Thinking too hard?" he teased, then, with effort pinched his lips into a straight line when she glared at him.

Even when he was furious, she made him want to grin like the cat who swallowed the canary.

"Who else could it be?"

Her query echoed his own, the question which had plagued him all afternoon, ever since he'd spoken to Ellis's grandmother.

"According to his grandmother, Ellis flew off to Wyoming three days ago," he explained, his voice gruff.

"She could be lying," Dixie suggested.

Erik barked out a laugh. "Whatever kind of boy

Ellis turned out to be, it's not his grandmother's fault. She's a saint. Trust me. She's not lying.''

He glanced in her direction to see how she was taking the news. Her face looked pale, and her eyebrows were scrunched over her nose. She looked like a little girl who was concentrating too hard on a new, foreign task.

He probably wasn't all that far from the truth.

Granted, she was no little girl. She'd turned into a beautiful woman, inside and out. But her mind must be swirling with conflicting thoughts, and none of them pleasant.

''Who else could it be?'' she demanded, sounding as if she expected him to have an answer.

What infuriated him was that he *didn't* have the answer. He hadn't found time to follow up on John Needleson, and was no closer to solving the mystery of the unknown vandal than when he'd begun.

Who else cared whether or not Dixie stayed on the land? And why stoop to vandalism to make a point?

He hadn't thought Ellis to be so foolish, for all his bluster, and he'd been right. His gut instinct served him well in that case. But this same instinct was blaring now, telling him more, warning him that what they faced—what Dixie faced—was more dangerous than a mere adolescent on the rampage.

A man vandalizing for vandalism's sake, or out to get his kicks, didn't leave warning messages.

"How well do you know John Needleson?" he barked.

"John? Why do you ask?"

He cringed inwardly at the informal use of Needleson's name. Irritated, he pinned her with a look that said *Just tell me.*

She shrugged. "I don't. I called every number in the newspaper advertising horses for sale. As soon as he heard my name, he really perked up. He must have realized we were neighbors. Anyway, he told me he thought he had the ideal horse for me."

Erik frowned. He'd been suspicious the day Dixie brought Victory home, and now warning sirens were screaming in his head.

John Needleson had been in horses all his life. He knew better than to sell a new rider a green broke yearling.

Unless he was doing it on purpose. And from what Dixie said, it sounded like John knew exactly what he was doing.

Putting Dixie in danger.

He kicked himself for not realizing it earlier. John Needleson was a threat to Dixie. And his gut told him John was the man behind the vandalism.

The only question was *Why?*

"How did he act when you were over there?" he asked through clenched teeth.

Her gaze darted to his, but he hooded his look so he wouldn't give anything away.

"He was friendly," she began, staring down at her fingers, which were laced tightly in her lap. "A little withdrawn, maybe. But his wife passed away recently."

"Two years ago."

She frowned, the light leaving her eyes for a split second before she regrouped. "Sometimes love is so strong it lasts forever."

Ouch. That hurt.

He swallowed hard, dislodging the lump in his throat. Her message couldn't be more clear if she'd stamped it on the dashboard.

"Go on," he said when he'd recovered from the unspoken blow.

"I don't know what this has to do with anything," she objected, her voice as sharp as a needle.

"Humor me."

"Well, we talked about Victory. And a little about his wife, although he shied away from the subject." He heard the catch in her throat. "I tried to make an overture of friendship, with us being near neighbors and all, but he didn't seem ready to accept it."

Yeah, he'd just bet John wasn't after friendship. He had always been crotchety.

"Which is odd," she said, sounding perplexed.

He tensed. "Why is that?"

"Because when I offered for him to visit the retreat, he pretty much promised he would."

Erik's grip tightened on the steering wheel.

John had visited, all right. With a bowie knife.

But the question lingered, one that he was certain would keep him up nights until he figured the answer to the riddle.

Why would John Needleson care one way or another about Dixie's retreat?

Dixie called it an early night and tucked herself in her room at the lodge. She'd already put her own finishing touches on her personal space.

Keeping with the rustic theme, she'd decorated with old-fashioned quilted patterns on everything from the curtains to the nightstand to the oversize comforter draping her twin bed. She liked the result so much she was considering doing all the bedrooms in the lodge in a similar style.

If she could get to town to buy the necessary materials before something else bad happened. It was a good thing she didn't believe in bad luck, because it appeared to be following her with a vengeance these days.

She'd always been an optimist, with her faith in God as a basis for seeing the glass half-full. But the past few months had taken their toll on her. She was exhausted, both physically and mentally.

The glass looked precariously empty at the moment.

Erik's accusation that John Needleson was behind

the vandalism stayed with her, despite her original inclination to disregard it.

Had John purposely sold her a horse she couldn't ride in order to endanger her? How could that be? Her run-in with him in town seemed to confirm her suspicions, but she still couldn't figure out why his animosity was being shined in her direction.

It was true he hadn't exactly welcomed her with open arms when she'd visited him, but then again, she'd seen the vulnerability beneath his tough exterior, empathized with his grief over the loss of his beloved wife.

And it *was* the first time they'd met.

John might be bitter, but he had no reason to take it out on Dixie. And as far as the horse went, she didn't recall informing him of her level of experience regarding horsemanship. He'd probably naturally assumed her to be an expert.

Brushing thoughts of vandalism aside, she turned her mind to her biggest problem. A walking, seldom talking, often brooding, sometimes laughing package of trouble, with a capital T.

Erik Wheeler.

It was time to stop avoiding the obvious and face up to the truth. Erik had become her right-hand man, and more than that, her dearest friend.

And now she was experiencing feelings she'd never thought to encounter in her lifetime—and certainly not as compelling and emotion laden as they were.

She'd once thought herself to be in love with Abel, but now she questioned those feelings. She'd been young and idealistic, and Abel offered everything she thought she wanted.

But her love for Abel had been soft, soothing. If it was love at all. She'd never experienced with him the depth of response she felt with Erik. Abel never made her heart leap out of her chest and her mind sing praises to God.

Abel was not a lover. Not as a husband should be.

The truth was, she'd been a young woman trying to escape her father's heavy hand. It troubled her now to realize she might have lived her whole life without knowing the kind of passion Erik instilled in her.

She would have settled for second best.

The realization didn't hurt nearly as much as she would have expected. Perhaps she'd always known. As Abel had known.

She remembered his parting words, how much they'd torn her in two at the time. Now, she finally understood what he was trying to say.

You're not in love with me. Go to South Dakota. Find God's best for yourself.

He'd known. He'd understood how she had seen him, yet she'd filled a need in his life, as well.

She waited for her heart to fill with grief, with the sense of rejection she repeatedly tried to deny, but no pain occurred. Nothing flowed in her heart but peace, and for the first time, she could look back on her relationship with Abel with open eyes and a clear heart.

Her time with Abel had been so short. She'd first seen him at a local missions conference, speaking on his work in Pakistan as a tent maker. She'd been enthralled by his tales, and by the tall, thickly built blonde who'd dedicated his life to such a tough task.

Afterward, she'd spoken to him about her own mission dream in South Dakota. He'd encouraged her in it, and asked if he could call her sometime.

Less than twenty-four hours passed before he'd called and asked her to dinner. It only took one date to discover how much they had in common, and before she knew it, they were engaged and approaching their denomination about the work in South Dakota.

And then the politics of South Asia went into chaos, and Abel felt compelled to go and help. She couldn't stop him, nor would she have wanted to.

Maybe she knew all along his true place was in South Asia. Maybe she'd known all along she would only be with Abel for a time.

A season for everything, the Word said. Who was she to argue with the Bible?

Abel encouraged her to pursue her work here in

Custer. She'd even had a letter from him, detailing his work in Pakistan and inquiring about her work here at the retreat.

She smiled softly, though no one was there to see it. Funny how the pain of her loss had lost its sharp edges, becoming almost a comfort to her instead of distress.

Abel would approve of all she'd done. He would like Erik, just as she did.

No, that wasn't quite right.

What she felt for Erik—friendship, respect and appreciation—those things Abel would share. But there was a part of her heart that responded to Erik as a man, and she harbored that deep in her heart, cherishing the feeling, sharing it with no one else.

Up until now she hadn't even dared admit it openly to herself.

And it confused her. She'd never felt this way with Abel. His soft kiss made her feel warm and comfortable.

A mere look from Erik sent her heart into fits.

But how could two loves be so different? Her love for Erik was based on common interests, just as with Abel. But maturity gave her extra insight this time around.

She wasn't dependent on Erik, though the day wasn't complete without having him at her side.

She'd leaned on Abel, let him do the difficult tasks in starting a new mission, while she rode on his coattails. And when the going got tough, he rejected her.

No wonder she bristled every time Erik did anything for her. She wanted something different with him, something more than a platonic relationship that would have been convenient for all concerned.

It still bothered her that she had to depend on anyone—especially a man—to complete her work here. She knew it was her pride speaking, and she inwardly cringed as guilt washed over her.

She did depend on Erik.

She naturally turned to him with her problems. But he likewise turned to her. Hadn't he been talking with her more and more often?

That alone was a minor miracle. Was this what a mature love relationship was all about?

She didn't have the opportunity to pursue that question as someone knocked rapidly on her door, which led to an outside landing. The landing was graced by a small porch complete with an old wooden rocking chair for watching the mountain sunsets.

"Who is it?" she called, not bothering to rise from the edge of her bed.

"Erik."

She tensed. He'd never come to her room before, and she couldn't imagine why he'd be here now. Unless there was a problem.

More vandalism?

Chapter Sixteen

Dixie's heart jumped into her throat as she launched off the bed, not even habitually running an open palm across the comforter to straighten the wrinkles, as was in her perfectionist nature to do.

"What's wrong?" she demanded as she swung the door open without the pretense of a greeting.

Erik leaned his forearm against the doorframe and leaned toward her, his lips curling up in the corners just enough to suggest a smile. "Something have to be wrong for a man to visit a pretty lady?"

The skin on her face flushed with warmth under his scrutiny. She swore she'd never heard so many words from Erik before, except when he was talking to his beloved horses.

And he'd called her "pretty"!

"Well, no. I suppose not," she squeaked. She

swallowed, trying to regain her normal voice before she was forced to speak again.

With his free hand, he tipped his hat. "I have the team hitched."

"To the hay wagon?"

His blue eyes twinkled under the shadow of his black hat.

What else? he asked without speaking.

Her face went from warm to scorching. Of course, the team would be hitched to the hay wagon. It was the only wagon the retreat owned.

"Let's go," he said in his usual gruff way, but it was more a question than a command.

"Okay," she agreed, not having to think twice about learning to drive a team—or spending time with Erik.

"Oh, wait!" she exclaimed, trying to gather her wits about her. She scrambled back toward her knotted-pine dresser where a stack of horse books lay in a haphazard pile. She quickly sifted through them, at last finding the one she sought.

"Here," she said, waving the book in the air like a trophy. "We'll be needing this."

Erik cocked an eyebrow but said nothing. Still, she could see laughter in his eyes.

Which was nice, for a change, and she didn't care if she put it there, or more accurately, *how* she put it there.

He was too often broody. Laughter would be good for him, even if he kept it locked inside.

She'd show him just how much a person could learn from a book. She'd studied this particular book with extra attention, and felt quite certain—especially with the new hands-on horse knowledge she'd received from Erik—she could handle a team the first time out.

She knew the lines, and she knew the lingo. She smiled, secretly anticipating surprising Erik with her wisdom.

She exclaimed in delight when she saw the black-and-white Border collie in the back of the hay wagon.

Her angel!

"This here's Lucy," Erik said, hoping to keep the introduction short.

"Lucy is *your* dog?"

Lucy. She should have known.

"Yep."

"I see." She greeted the dog with the enthusiasm she didn't want to show Lucy's owner. But she supposed nothing bad had come from his little deletion. And she'd missed Lucy's company since she had moved into the main lodge.

His mouth was still crooked in a semigrin when he lifted her onto the buckboard, his large hands spanning her waist. A thousand little darts of electricity bolted through her, and it wasn't an entirely unpleasant sensation. Her head swam with the delicious feeling.

"This one's Cindy, and that there is Suzy," he introduced, pointing at the horses left to right. When they heard their names, the horses fidgeted in their harnesses.

"Cindy and Suzy. How lovely."

She admired the matched pair of palomino mares. Suzy was darker than Cindy, but other than that, they were a perfectly matched team.

"They're full sisters," he explained.

"I wondered how they looked so much alike."

Erik's grin cracked through to a smile. "Yep."

"Cindy and Suzy," she said again, liking how it made the horses' ears perk up. "And I should always call them left to right."

He conceded her small victory with a tug on his hat, which served only to shadow the amusement in his eyes.

She smiled and took up the lines, careful to lace them up between her pinkie and fourth finger and down between her thumb and first finger of each hand, just as the book illustrated.

He grunted, which, she supposed, was the closest she'd get to him telling her how impressed he was with her knowledge.

Excitement welling, she snapped the lines over the horses' backs, calling *"Git up!"* in her best John Wayne voice.

Cindy and Suzy didn't move an inch with her command, and neither did the wagon. Chagrined, she flushed heatedly and darted a glance at Erik.

He didn't so much as blink as he leaned back into the seat and put his arm around the back. "Talk 'em through it," he suggested quietly. "Use their names."

"Of course," she snapped back, though his only crime was being his usual kind self. The truth was she was annoyed with herself for forgetting what she'd learned so quickly.

Use the horses' names. Any idiot would know that. And there was something about calling left and right hovering at the top of her brain somewhere just out of reach.

Oh, yes. The commands.

Straightening her spine, she darted another glance at Erik and cleared her throat.

Let's try this again.

"Cindy, *come gee.* Suzy, *go haw!*"

The horses twitched in anticipation when she called their names, and to her delight the cart lurched at the same time her heart did.

For about one second.

After that, both the wagon and her heart died down to a standstill. She wanted to scream in frustration.

Instead, she sighed loudly and glared at Erik as if

he were the cause of the problem. She knew she was being irrational, and she didn't care.

"What now?" she grumbled, making a meager attempt to keep her voice level.

He gestured toward her book. "That thing tell you to do this?"

She glanced down at the book in her lap and nodded. "Yes. I mean, well, I think it did."

"That so," he replied, definitely amused.

"Why? What did I do wrong?"

He chuckled. "For starters, you just told the horses to switch places. A little difficult with them being harnessed up and all."

She scowled, then gave it up and broke out in a laugh despite herself. "Poor things. I really confused them, didn't I?"

He shrugged. "They'll get over it."

"I must have gotten it backward. I thought you were supposed to call them something left to right."

"Their names. Haw and Gee are directions—*go* left and right."

"Oh," she said, deflated. She unlaced the lines and tossed them toward Erik. "You want to take over?"

The twinkle in his eye turned into a hard gleam as he swung his arm over her head and snatched up the lines, immediately lacing them through his rough and tethered hands.

"What did I do wrong now?" she asked, thoroughly exasperated with the entire experience.

He frowned down at her. "You let go of the lines."

"Of course I did. How else could I hand them to you?"

He shrugged. "And what if the horses had bolted? Those lines would be long gone by now. You and I would be eating dust."

"Oh." She hadn't thought of that, and certainly her worthless book hadn't mentioned such a possibility.

This was supposed to be an easy transition from regular riding to team driving.

Easy, ha!

She'd botched it up, just as she'd bungled every other project she'd attempted since coming to South Dakota. Another tent falling on top of her, and this time Erik was here to see it and laugh at her mistakes. Although at the moment, he wasn't laughing.

"I just thought you'd want to take over," she retorted sharply.

Like you always do.

His gaze met hers, probing and searching. Or was it teasing? She couldn't tell, with the brim of his hat shading his eyes.

"You thought wrong." He offered her the lines, which she accepted after considering his shadowed expression a moment longer.

Erik let her look her fill, knowing she couldn't read what was really in his heart. He'd turned away from her a hundred times, and a hundred times she'd turned him back, made him face the demons haunting him.

It was better for a man just to come clean with Dixie. She always wriggled the truth out of him anyway. He admired her spirit, just as he admired everything else about the small, plucky woman.

"You've got the left-to-right part down," he explained awkwardly. When she frowned and creased her forehead in that little-girl concentrating look she had, he decided once again that words were useless. At least to him they were.

Clamping his mouth shut, he showed her how to strip the lines shorter in her hands without letting go of either piece of worn leather.

"This will give you more control," he said after several minutes, when she appeared to have mastered command of the lines.

She nodded, still concentrating furiously.

"Relax," he coaxed, just as he had when she learned to ride Victory.

Dixie took everything way too seriously, especially horses. "This won't be much different than riding. Cindy and Suzy have been a team for years now."

She blew out a breath and visibly relaxed her posture. The movement caused the book on her lap to slide to the side, lodging next to Erik's thigh.

With a chuckle, he picked up the book, waving it in front of her nose. *"How to Drive a Team in Five Easy Lessons?"* he teased, though the actual title was something far less innocuous.

"Team Driving for Dummies," she countered with a laugh.

He slid a finger down the soft, peaches-and-cream skin of her cheek, then chucked her lightly underneath the chin. "You're no dummy."

She smiled, though a shadow passed over her face. "Thank you."

"So, are you gonna drive this team, or are we just going to sit out on this old hay wagon all night?"

"Cindy, Suzy, git up!" This time, the horses sprang forward, causing them both to lurch back in their seats.

"Still have the lines tight?" he asked, adjusting his position and replacing his arm behind her back. For reassurance, he assured himself, and not just because it felt good to put his arm around her.

"Yep," she said in an exact imitation of his low drawl.

"You sound like a regular cowboy," he teased.

She smiled hesitantly, and then her eyes grew wide as the horses lumbered toward the pasture, apparently taking it upon themselves to choose a route.

"What trail are we taking?" she squeaked, her voice high and tight.

Erik pointed to the left, where a wagon trail had been etched from the land by the stable hands. "That one there will take us to the steak."

"I wish." He heard the rumble of her stomach, offering its own opinion on the many benefits of a thick steak dinner.

"No supper?" he queried lightly.

She shook her head, and he struggled to keep his lips firm when they wanted to slide into a grin. Maybe he'd really surprise her, for once, with something nice, something she wouldn't take offense to. Maybe he was finally figuring the woman out.

But he wouldn't bet his paycheck on it.

"If you don't tell me how to turn this thing, we're going to be taking another route, right into that tree up there," she said, her voice teasing, if tight.

"Cindy, Suzy, *go haw,*" he said, turning his attention to the horses, who immediately followed his command, moving to the left and toward the correct trail.

"How did you do that?" she demanded, glancing curiously at him. "I thought the one with the lines did the driving."

He just shrugged, afraid he'd ruined the moment with his casual instructions, which came second nature to him.

"You drive them with your voice?" she persisted when he didn't answer.

He shrugged again. "Mostly."

"Teach me," she pleaded, her voice low and earnest. "I want to learn."

Her insatiable need to learn was one of the things he loved most about Dixie. He was one cowboy who thought he was beyond learning new tricks, but she'd proven him wrong, again and again.

"You know most of it. Use their names. *Gee* for right, *haw* for left. *Go* for forward, *come* for back."

"That's all?"

"Pretty much." He gestured to the driving whip posted in one corner. "Some people direct their horses with a whip."

"A whip? Isn't that rather barbaric?"

She sounded truly affronted, and he chuckled. "Not really. You don't actually whip the horses. Just touch their flanks to let 'em know where to go."

"Oh. I see," she said, sounding like she didn't *see* at all.

Erik couldn't stop smiling. Without realizing it, Dixie was lightly handling the lead lines, guiding the team down the trail.

"I think I'll just stick to using my voice and not a whip," she said at last.

He watched as she maneuvered the team over a small creek without so much as a whinny from either horse. She was a natural and she wasn't even aware of it. If only she knew.

Pride swelled in his chest, though there was no good reason for it. He sure couldn't take any credit for her natural talent and her unwavering willingness to try and try again until she got it right.

Clearing the frog from his throat, he turned his attention to the book in his hands. "Can't believe someone wrote a book on how to drive horses."

She glanced at him, a smile in her eyes, then returned her attention to the team, still a little too stiff in her movements, as if she were afraid of doing the wrong thing. "They have books on just about everything."

"I suppose they do," he said, astounded. He flipped through the pages, noting the illustrations. "Hey, look how this guy is holding the lines."

She leaned her cheek on his shoulder in order to see the picture he was pointing at, and he inhaled a large whiff of peaches from her hair. He closed his eyes for a moment, savoring the strong, sweet scent.

He was glad he wasn't driving. He'd probably land the wagon in a gully.

"They explain how to hold the lines correctly," she said, using her elbow to point to the man's hands. "But this guy is doing it one-handed, and with four horses instead of just two!"

He leaned his head in toward hers until they were both hunched over the book, laughing as he turned the pages to find other pictures of the one-handed team driver.

"Look at that one," she said, laughing and pointing to another picture. "He looks like he's going to go straight through that fence."

"He probably did," Erik replied gruffly. "What's he supposed to do if one of his horses balks?"

"I don't know. I can't even see how he could *hold* all those lines in one hand. I've got two hands full with only two horses." She sniffed in mock disdain. "You'd think a how-to manual like this one would—"

Her words cut off abruptly as she glanced up.

Erik's gaze followed hers. Their laughter turned into simultaneous gasps of breath as the horses headed straight into a copse of trees.

"Oh, no," Dixie exclaimed, pulling hard on the lines. "Whoa, Cindy, whoa, Suzy. Good girls."

Erik had to bite the inside of his lip to keep from laughing, but he knew instinctively that was the *last* thing he should do right now.

Dixie would laugh about her circumstances later, but not right now, not while they were headed into heavy wood and toward the streambed. Her forehead was already creased with exertion.

"Cindy, Suzy," he said, hoping Dixie wouldn't be too angry with him for helping out once again. "*Come gee.* Easy now. That's it, darlins."

The horses, calmed by the tenor of Erik's voice,

backed slowly until they reached the point they'd left the track.

"*Git up,* girls," Dixie said, her voice tight, as she directed them back to the trail. "That's the way."

Erik sat with his hands in his lap, gripping the book, unsure what to say, but pretty sure she was mad at him again.

At least until she flashed him a grateful smile.

"I'm glad you're with me," she admitted, her gaze fixed on the trail ahead of them.

She sounded almost shy, Erik thought, amazed. The same woman who would take on a mountain, and she was being shy around him.

It couldn't be because…no. He stopped that thought before it formed.

Dixie was off-limits to a rough-and-tumble cowboy like he was. But that didn't stop him from wanting to see her happy, wanting to know he'd been the one to place the smile on her face.

"This is the spot," he said suddenly.

Dixie, her mind thoroughly occupied keeping the team on an even keel over the bumpy trail, looked up, startled. "The spot for what?"

He couldn't be talking about the steak dinner area, because she knew that area had been cleared and settled with picnic tables, a barbecue pit and a large, central campfire.

Given that, they obviously hadn't yet reached the end of the trail.

She glanced at him with raised eyebrows, but didn't make the mistake of locking gazes with him this time.

"Just pull over."

And stop asking questions.

It was usually what he didn't say that meant so much more than the words that came out of his mouth.

"All right, already," she said, protesting, as she coaxed the horses to a halt.

Erik rolled off the buckboard and reached his hands up to her. "Come on."

She gestured to the lines still laced through her hands. "What am I supposed to do with these?"

He tipped his hat off his head and tossed it into the back of the wagon, his eyes gleaming.

What, your book didn't tell you that?

She narrowed her gaze on him. "I obviously need some help here."

Obviously.

But he didn't say it aloud. He never did.

Instead, he reached up and unlaced the lines, then set the wooden brake and looped the lines around it.

"Now will you get down?"

He raised his arms again, but she ignored them, choosing to jump off the buckboard on her own.

She landed hard, but pride kept her from saying *ouch* when her right ankle turned underneath her.

She pulled her mouth into a hard straight line against the pain.

"I'm down. Now will you tell me what we're doing in the meadow, out in the middle of nowhere?"

Despite her actions to the contrary, he obviously noticed her distress. He leapt to her side and took her arm. "Easy on that leg."

Before she could protest, he'd swept her into his arms and was tramping across the bright-green meadow, which, she noticed as she laid her cheek against the musky, rough flannel of Erik's shirt, was in full bloom with a contrast of wildflowers of every size, shape and color.

A lovely place for a picnic. If only she'd remembered she hadn't eaten dinner and had thought to pack some food along.

Her stomach growled. She felt Erik's chest move as he chuckled, though she couldn't hear a sound. He even laughed silently.

Affronted, she tensed. "I told you I didn't eat dinner," she said, trying not to sound huffy.

"You shouldn't treat your stomach that way. It's protesting."

"Well, there's not much I can do about it out here in the middle of nowhere, now is there?"

He looked down at her and grinned. "I wouldn't be so sure about that."

Her breath caught in her throat at the same moment her gaze caught his.

Intense. Yearning. Teasing. It was all there, and more.

That brief glimpse into his soul was more than enough to make her try to wriggle from his grasp, twisted ankle or no twisted ankle. Her skin felt warm and tingly, and her heart beat an erratic tempo in her throat, which completely ruled out the possibility of breathing.

She wasn't ready to confront the emotions she felt.

And neither, it appeared, was Erik, for he didn't struggle against her, but released her onto the soft grass underneath a thick lodgepole pine. Lucy joined her under the tree, curling up against her side and promptly falling asleep.

"Stay put," he said, his voice unusually low and husky. Apparently, she wasn't the only one struggling to be casual when she felt anything but.

Rubbing her right ankle, which she noticed absently was beginning to swell, she watched Erik walk back across the meadow to the hay wagon.

What an incredible man he was, outside as well as inside. He was a Western woman's wildest fantasy, a combination of every cowboy hero she'd ever seen on television and then some.

Except the real thing was so much better.

She would never have believed such strength and

gentleness could reside within the same body, especially in a man. Yet Erik was just that—a rough-edged cowboy with the kindest heart she'd ever known.

Her heart hammered against her ribs. For once, she was able to see the things he did for her through his eyes. Even now, hiking back across the meadow with a picnic basket in one hand and brown woolen blanket folded over his other arm, his expression was a peculiar combination of eagerness and anxiousness.

He probably thought she was going to read him the riot act for doing yet another project without asking her permission first.

And he was probably right, under usual circumstances. What a mother hen she was becoming! She didn't have a clue why she was so churlish with him.

He certainly didn't deserve it. She knew deep down in her heart everything he did, he did for her.

Like giving her this much-needed break. He was a man of action, not of words, and no amount of nagging on her part was going to change that. He'd seen what needed to be done, and he did it, no questions asked.

But she saw his jaw tense as he approached. "I brought dinner."

It was a lovely surprise, and for once Dixie took it at face value. Also for the first time, she was going to surprise him, as well.

"That was very thoughtful, Erik. Thank you."

While he stood staring and groped for words, she reached for the blanket and unfolded it, allowing him to help her slide into a comfortable position on it before she took the proffered basket.

"Nothing much," he protested with a shrug.

"Yes, it is." She smiled up at him and patted the blanket next to her. "Sit down, and let's see what we can do about taking that growl away from my stomach."

He dropped to his knees beside her, his dark hair creased where his hat had been. He scrubbed a hand over his scalp when he noticed the direction of her gaze.

"Should have cleaned up first."

"For a picnic? Nonsense." She scrubbed a hand along her own scalp, knowing she was doing far more damage to her hairstyle than he'd done to his. "Besides, the windblown look is in these days."

He barked out a laugh and reached for the fried chicken leg she offered him. It was like music to hear him laugh, though she suspected he had more humor inside than he often let show. She was glad he could loosen up some around her.

"Did you go on many picnics as a kid? Church picnics? Family picnics? Extended family picnics?" she asked, thinking he wasn't really the picnicking type.

His face shadowed with pain. "No."

She put a hand on his forearm, feeling the tension there. "I'm sorry. I've obviously stumbled on a touchy subject. Forget I said anything. I don't want to ruin our lovely picnic."

He smiled, but she could tell it was forced. "It's okay, really. My mother..." He looked away across the meadow for a moment. The silence was broken only by the sound of the birds in their summer glory.

"You don't have to talk about it."

His gaze flashed back to her. "Yes I do. My mother used to read the Bible every evening to us, right before bed. She made us go to church and Sunday school. And church picnics."

"What happened?"

He looked down at the blanket and began picking small specks of grass from it and shaking them away. "She died in childbirth with my youngest brother when I was eight."

Raw pain pierced her heart as she saw the hurt little boy in his eyes.

"My father didn't know how to go on without her, so he just pretty much ignored us boys."

"Boys?"

"There are three of us. I'm the oldest, then Ethan. Everett—Rhett—is the baby. I had to take care of them because Dad wouldn't." He lifted her hand from his arm and laced his fingers with hers.

She was glad for the comfort he drew from her.

And it certainly explained why he was so angry at God.

Dear Lord, You're the only one who can help him, she prayed, her heart nearly breaking in two.

Their gazes met, and he smiled softly, genuinely this time. "I'm just glad to be here with you," he admitted.

"Me, too," she agreed, choking on the words.

Glad. And scared out of her wits.

She and Erik were getting closer, which was something she was infinitely happy about. Yet it also caused her more sorrow than if she'd never met him in the first place.

The closer they became, the more Dixie saw the potential for a romantic relationship between them—and the more worried she became. A serious problem had been haunting her now for weeks.

Erik didn't know the Lord.

It was a gap that no human could breech. For if he didn't know her Savior, he could never *really* know her. Not really.

Not forever.

Chapter Seventeen

A full week later, Dixie still limped on her ankle, though the swelling had gone down considerably. Starting as a glaring purplish-red, it had faded to a dull, dark-lilac color.

Erik had insisted she stay off her feet for the first couple of days, but there was too much left to do before her church friends arrived to keep her down for long.

Less than a week left, and the real test would begin. She didn't know whether it was a blessing or a curse that the first guests visiting the lodge were people she knew intimately.

Gritting her teeth against the pain, she limped toward the kitchen, wanting to go over the menu with James one last time, just to double-check that they had everything they needed when their guests arrived.

She was more nervous and worried than she cared to admit. What if her church guests were disappointed?

It wasn't inconceivable that the denomination could pull their support if they received a bad report and had reason to believe the work she'd done thus far wasn't being carried out to their standards.

But the people from her home church in Denver were her friends, the ones who'd stood behind her when Abel returned to Pakistan, the ones who helped convince the denominational leaders they could trust her to do this job alone.

And she *had* done it alone.

Well, maybe not *alone,* she amended mentally. God had sent her Erik, and together they had transformed the ragged land into a peaceful mountain retreat. Surely her guests could grow close to God here, just as she had.

But Erik hadn't.

Strong, silent Erik, who would no more talk about God than he'd grow antlers and a tail. Erik, the man dearest to her heart of all her staff, the man she'd prayed most earnestly for.

Erik had every reason not to trust God. All the more reason to seek Him.

Yet it hadn't happened, not so much as a hint that he was more open to a relationship with God. He'd accepted the New Testament she offered with nothing stronger than a noncommittal grunt, which coincided with him slipping it into the breast pocket of his Western shirt and out of sight.

He hadn't even cracked it open to see the inscription she'd written inside.

Shaking those depressing thoughts away, she entered the dining room, inhaling the sweet aroma of fresh-baked corn bread. Her mouth watered, and she realized once again she hadn't been eating regular meals.

Dinner wasn't for an hour yet, and suddenly she was ravenous. She wondered if James would allow her to sample a piece of his prized bread early.

"James?" Her voice echoed through the A-frame dining hall. "That corn bread smells delicious."

The burly cook blasted backward through the swinging double doors between the dining hall and the kitchen, his arms loaded with dishes. "Give me a minute and I'll get you some," he said, his expression tight with concentration as he performed his balancing act.

"I'll do one better. Let me help," Dixie offered with a laugh, moving forward to take a stack of freshly washed plates from his arms.

James shifted the remaining plates and bowls as she carefully cradled her own.

"Where do you want them?"

James nodded to the table.

"Fire!"

The male voice came from the back door, followed by a series of frantic thumps that Dixie recognized as pounding fists on wood.

An alarm.

"Fire! The stable is on fire!" the voice screamed again, frantic.

"Erik!" Dixie shrieked as her pile of plates slid from her grasp and went crashing to the floor. "Oh, Lord, help me," she prayed aloud. "The horses!"

Dixie covered her mouth with her hand, her gaze darting from the door to James, to the pile of now-dirty plastic plates on the floor. She tried to speak, but only gibberish came from her throat.

Her heart pounded frantically in her head as she brought her gaze back up to James, apologizing with a look, and hoping she didn't look anywhere near as hysterical as she felt.

He gestured with his head, waving her off. "Go see to Erik. And the horses," he said, as if it were an afterthought. "I'll clean up here."

For a moment, she couldn't think, couldn't move. Then adrenaline shot through her, thawing her frozen limbs and numb mind, charging her into action.

Erik! The horses!

She limped out the door without looking back. General hysteria reigned in the yard, with various staff members dashing this way and that, running in every direction. Some toted buckets of water, others the handmade quilts from their own beds.

And everyone was yelling.

It was hard to determine what was happening. She couldn't see Erik anywhere. But he'd be in the stable, with the horses.

Lord, keep him safe.

It looked like smoke was coming from behind the stable, and she couldn't see any flames from her present position. Nor did she see any horses.

Someone would be rescuing them.

Erik.

Where were the stable hands?

She faltered. Should she go into the stable? Look for the foundation of the fire? Two of James's kitchen helpers dashed by her and around the backside of the stable, each toting buckets slopping full of water.

Fire.

Her breath coming in shallow gasps, she pinched her fingers over the cramp in her side and followed the kitchen staff with the buckets.

As soon as she rounded the corner, flames filled her view, shooting sky-high, just as smoke filled her nostrils, throat and lungs, making her gag. Her eyes watered until she could barely see.

She blinked once. Twice. And mercifully her gaze found Erik.

Thank You, God.

She stumbled toward him, wondering vaguely why he wasn't dashing back and forth like everyone else on the planet.

But, of course, Erik wouldn't panic. That wasn't his way.

He stood quietly, his booted feet braced, his hands fisted on his hips. An aggressive, angry stance from any distance, though he didn't move a muscle.

She knew he didn't see her coming, but she flung her arms around him nonetheless, laying her cheek against the breadth of his back. He was so strong.

Invulnerable, almost. She drew strength from him as a river drew its strength from the ocean.

"The horses?" she croaked through a smoke-dry throat.

Erik turned his gaze to her, his eyes nearly black with rage. He pinched his lips together before answering. "The horses are fine, Dixie."

"But the fire—"

"Was confined to our summer supply of hay."

"The stable?" Reassured by Erik's words, she leaned her palms on her knees, forcing her breath to slow as oxygen stung her lungs every time she inhaled.

"The fire was well planned. There's no danger to any of the buildings, or to the horses."

"And no one was injured?"

He shook his head.

"Thank God," she whispered.

"Thank *God?*" he echoed, sounding astounded and out-of-his-wits angry. "For *what?*"

She narrowed her eyes on him.

He clenched his jaw and looked away.

As anger replaced fear, Dixie stomped toward the fire, assessing the damage.

She found it to be just as Erik said. The fire was well controlled. At Erik's insistence, their hay supply was stacked away from the stable.

If she remembered correctly, she'd argued with him over how much more work was involved hauling hay from a distance, but he'd stubbornly insisted. What wouldn't fit in the extra space inside the stable was stacked on a small hill of dirt and gravel and covered with a tarp.

Now the hay was all gone. But because of Erik's foresight, no one had been hurt, and the self-contained fire would eventually die out on its own and affect none of the buildings.

Again, she thanked God, knowing His hand was in this, keeping her and all those she was responsible for in safety.

It could have been worse. Much worse.

She felt rather than saw Erik walk up behind her, and tensed as he laid a hand on her shoulder.

"How did it happen?" she asked quietly when he didn't say a word.

"It wasn't an accident."

She whirled on him. "What?"

She didn't know what she expected—there hadn't been a thunderstorm for lightning to have struck, nor any children who might be playing with matches.

Teenagers smoking behind the haystack?

Maybe.

She looked up into Erik's smoldering eyes. Or maybe not.

"This was a warning. Someone set this fire on purpose."

She shook her head, wanting to deny what her intuition said was true. "How do you know?"

He thumped his stomach with the palm of his hand. "My gut."

She turned back to the blazing fire and wrapped her arms around herself, shivering against the sudden chill his words brought. Or maybe it was that long drawl she'd learned to trust.

"Look," he said, pointing to a trench that had been dug around the rim of the haystack.

She frowned, concentrating. Erik hadn't ordered a trench to be dug around the pile—she would have remembered that. And the dirt looked freshly turned.

Peculiar.

Whoever started the fire had gone to a lot of trouble to leave her with nothing more than an expensive bonfire, not a life-threatening forest fire.

He, or she, was making a statement. So much for the smoking teenager theory.

The bowie knife used to slash her tires flashed into her mind, and she shivered.

No accident.

"Is there any clue who did it?"

Erik grunted and shook his head. "Haven't had much of a chance to look."

He began another inspection of the perimeter of the fire, scowling at the ground as he went. Dixie ran a hand through her hair and blew out a breath. Her head ached from smoke and panic.

But she had to think.

If there was a note, as there had been last time, it wouldn't be in or even near the fire. The nearest building was the stable, so she turned around and started back up the hill the way she'd come, looking for she didn't know what.

Anything suspicious, she supposed. Some clue as to who might have started the fire.

Whoever slashed her tires wanted her to know how it was done, and why. She suspected this fire was no different.

She gasped as her gaze honed in on the gleam of a bowie knife stuck into a wood post that helped support the farthest corral.

The place Erik taught her to ride Victory. The sight of the knife slashed all her good memories, immediately replacing them with anger and fear.

The knot in her stomach tightened. A single sheet

of paper, pinned to the post with the knife, waved in the slight summer breeze.

No accident.

Erik stalked past her and directly to the knife, ripping the paper away from the post. He took one look, muttered something unintelligible under his breath and crumpled the note in his hand. Moments later, he tossed it at his feet.

Dixie scrambled for the paper, but Erik was faster, covering it with the heel of his boot.

"Give it to me," she demanded, pounding her fists against his booted calf.

He shrugged and held firm.

"Erik."

His boot moved a fraction of an inch, enough for her to get a good grip on the note, but not enough for her to pull it away without tearing it.

"Erik," she said again, hating the hint of pleading in her voice.

He stepped back and folded his arms over his chest, looking none too pleased to have complied.

She didn't care what he thought. She snatched the paper up before he had the opportunity to change his mind, and smoothed the creases out on her knee with her palm.

"Go home. You don't belong here."

Her heart tearing in two, she looked up at Erik, but he wouldn't meet her gaze. She swirled on her toes and sat down hard in the dirt. Her head spun with conflicting thoughts. The sharp gravel cut into her thighs, but she welcomed the pain as a means to regain her focus.

Slashed tires were one thing. But a fire?

Someone could have been hurt.

Why was John Needleson singling her out? What purpose could it possibly serve?

Someone could have been injured.

If the fire spread, everyone would have been in serious danger.

Erik. Tally. James. Victory. Not to mention her neighbors, and even the townsfolk of Custer itself.

She was putting them all in danger.

The consequences were clear, even if the truth was yet to be shown.

Erik yanked his hat off and crouched beside her, curling the brim in his hands. "Dixie, I..."

His gaze, loaded with warmth and compassion, locked with hers. He cleared his throat, then reached for her hand.

"I don't want to hear it," she snapped, afraid the tears burning in her eyes were going to slip down her face at any moment. Especially if Erik said something kind, and she knew he was going to do that very thing.

She pushed to her knees, then scrambled to her feet and beyond his reach. If there was one thing she couldn't handle right now, it was compassion.

She'd stomped away about five feet before Erik

caught up with her, clamping his hat on his head as he went. "Where are you going?"

She clenched her jaw, refusing to answer as she kept moving.

"Dixie," he pleaded, trying again.

She yanked on the door to her studio and walked in without a word. She needed to be alone to think.

He was right behind her.

She never expected him to follow her into her own room, but maybe it was just as well. He'd have to learn of her hastily made plans sooner or later.

She reached for her suitcase at the top of her closet and began cramming it full of jeans and sweaters from her dresser.

It was time for this city girl to go back to designer jeans and enamel-based fingernails.

Erik caught her arm and wheeled her about. "What are you doing?" he barked.

"What does it look like?" she spat back, yanking her arm from his grasp. "Doing what you—what *everyone*—has wanted me to do since the day I got here."

She pinned him with a glare, anchoring her roiling emotions. A solitary tear escaped down her cheek and she dashed it away.

"I'm leaving."

Chapter Eighteen

Dixie was serious.

Erik had seen her doubt herself a hundred times, and a hundred times he'd watched her pull herself up by her bootstraps, bolstered by her faith in God.

This time was different. He saw it in her eyes. She was going to leave.

Unless he stopped her.

"It was signed with a Bar N," he said, his voice low and even as if speaking to a spooked pony.

She swung on him, her aqua blue eyes flashing with hurt and anger. "What?"

"The note was signed," he repeated patiently.

"Bar N. John Needleson's brand."

He narrowed his eyes on her, anticipating her reaction. "Exactly."

"John Needleson started this fire." She didn't sound surprised, only weary and world-worn.

"And slashed your tires."

She dropped her gaze, then turned slowly back to her suitcase. Her shoulders rose and fell rapidly with her shallow breathing. He wanted to reach out to her, comfort her, reassure her.

Instead, he jammed his hands into the front pockets of his jeans. She didn't want his help.

"It doesn't make any difference," she said in a low monotone, her voice hollow.

"It makes *every* difference," Erik retorted darkly, glad his hands were in his pockets so he couldn't slam his fist into a wall in frustration.

"No."

"I'll see to Needleson myself," he vowed. Fury flared, lightning-hot and surging through his chest.

John Needleson put Dixie in danger. John Needleson was running her off her own land.

It wasn't going to happen.

Dixie stopped her edgy motion of packing and turned on Erik, gently laying her hands on his elbows as she looked up into his face. The scent of peaches emanated from her hair.

It was a dumb thing to notice at a time like this. But he couldn't help it, with her standing so close to him. What was a man to do?

He took a deep breath, trying to stabilize his suddenly jumpy nerves. He looked down at her tanned, no longer so peaches-and-cream complexion and those big aqua eyes staring back up at him, and knew he couldn't let her leave.

Dixie slid her hands from his elbows to his shoulders, feeling the tension in his muscles mounting. Anger shot like sparks from his eyes. She was shaking inside from rage, but knew she wouldn't act on it.

Erik, she wasn't so sure of.

"Why did He do this to you?" he growled, placing his hands over hers.

"John Needleson?"

"God."

He moved her arms around his neck and slipped his around her waist, pulling her tight. The smell of soap and leather was a soothing balm to Dixie, who burrowed farther into the softness of his shirt, such a contrast to the rock-hard muscle of the man underneath.

It was soothing, though his words were not. "What have you done to deserve this?"

"God didn't do this to me." She laughed shakily. "He's not some big old guy hanging out in heaven getting His kicks making us tiny little humans squirm."

He made a sound in his throat that could have been a chuckle. Dixie leaned back to see his face. He looked as broody as ever.

"How do you know?" He tipped his forehead

down until it was touching hers, his gaze serious. His breath was warm and sweet on her cheek, smelling lightly of cinnamon. "How do you even know He's there at all?"

"I know," she affirmed. "Here." She placed her hand over his heart.

"And here." She touched his temple. "I believe what the Bible says about who God is, and that's a loving Father."

Brushing the back of his hand across her cheek, she tucked her head into his chest. Silently he stroked her hair. His breathing was regular and even, soothing in its rhythm.

"He sent His Son to die on a cross for our sins, Erik. He couldn't possibly ask me to do anything more difficult than that."

He went as still as stone, not even breathing, and she was afraid she'd said too much. She didn't want to bully him into the Kingdom of God. She just wanted him to know it was there when he was ready to seek it.

"I'm sorry," she apologized, pushing away from him.

Being held by cold steel beams wasn't as comforting as the soft warmth Erik had provided earlier. "I won't leave. I promise."

He swung around, grabbed his hat from the bed and clamped it on his head. His lips were sealed in a firm, straight line, and his eyes were dark with anger.

Without a word to her, or even acknowledging she was there, Erik stalked out the door, slamming it behind him.

Was he still so angry with God? Or was John Needleson going to bear the brunt of his resentment?

She wasn't about to wait and see.

Erik knew he was being rude, but he had to escape the confines of her small studio. It smothered him, all of it.

The faint, tantalizing scent of peaches that lingered wherever Dixie was. The way she'd made her room a home, with little feminine touches his own mobile—he wouldn't even go so far as to call it a *home*—lacked completely.

And most of all her words of faith.

He was angry.

Terribly, violently angry. It pulsed through him, wild and hot. He wanted to punch a tree. He wanted to wring John Needleson's neck with his own bare hands.

And all the while, the lingering, empty ache in his chest grew larger and larger. He had the peculiar sense he was being pursued. Not by a human being, but by God Himself.

How could this be?

He squeezed his eyes shut. Up until recently, he

hadn't believed there was a God. And then he'd started reading that little New Testament, and the words had come alive in his heart.

Man shall not live by bread alone, but by every word that proceeds from the mouth of God.

He staggered through the trees, away from the compound. Toward his own land, where he was certain he could be alone.

It was ironic at a time like this, that he was running away in order to be alone, when he'd never felt more achingly alone—*lonely*—in his entire life.

Dixie's threat to leave just about undid him. He should be following up on his words and paying John Needleson a visit. But he knew he wouldn't. Not now, with anger and hate boiling over like lava, melting everything in its path.

At last he fell to his knees on a bed of pine needles just out of sight of his mobile.

"Oh, God." It was all he could think of to say. Emotions poured from his heart, all the hate and bitterness he'd stored up over the years. He didn't know what to do with emotion.

Feeling anything at all was foreign to him, at least until Dixie had come into his life with her strong-willed faith, uncorking the dam of emotions he'd tried so hard to keep hidden over the years. He could no more stop the whirling tempest of emotions consuming him than he could stop the tears from streaming down his face.

Dixie had opened his heart to the truth. She'd found a soft spot in his heart of stone. And Dixie's God—the God of the Bible—had whittled His way through.

"I'm sorry, God," he said aloud, not caring if someone overheard him. He felt as if the world had closed up for this one moment between him and God.

"I'm sorry for blaming You when my mother died. I'm sorry for not trusting You when You brought Dixie into my life."

He pounded his fists into the ground. "Help me to make things right. With You. And with her."

Swiping the tears from his eyes, he yanked the tiny New Testament from his breast pocket. He wanted to find that verse about the Word of God and read it again and again. Instead, he cracked the Bible open to the first page, and found there a dedication written in Dixie's stylish flair.

"The Lord be with you."

It was a short message, but enough to rock his world. He leaned his fists against the rough ground and held on for dear life. Waiting for he didn't know what.

God's spirit moved slowly and quietly as he sat bowed and broken under the tree, replacing hate and anger with love and peace.

And sheer, utter joy.

He felt as if someone had physically lifted a thousand-pound weight from his shoulders, and he almost wanted to sing, if he wasn't tone-deaf. He couldn't ever remember feeling so light and free. A verse from his childhood flew into his mind as if on wings.

Therefore if the Son makes you free, you shall be free indeed.

Finally he knew for certain, and wondered dazedly how he could have missed it all this time. Finally he understood the faith Dixie shared with him just by her life and example.

Had his father grown to understand this incomprehensible, yet amazingly simple truth? Is that why he'd left his ranch to the church and not to his son?

Was his father at peace now, by his mother's side in heaven?

Excitement coursed through him, and he laughed out loud. Joy as he'd never imagined pumped through his veins like adrenaline.

He wanted Dixie to be the first to know what had happened to this hardened cowboy's stone-cold heart.

It was alive and warm with the love of God.

Chapter Nineteen

Dixie waited a full fifteen minutes before asking for Victory to be brought around. She'd thought about taking her truck, but decided a straight shot through the trees would be faster.

Erik was on his way to see John Needleson, and she had to get there first. Or at least at the same time, which was all she could hope for.

She still didn't know why John—if it was John—had started that fire. But if he was angry with her for some reason, it sure wouldn't help to have Erik go running to her defense.

He was certainly angry enough to pick a fight. And if John Needleson was indeed the man behind the vandalism, he'd be ripe for the picking. Erik could be hurt.

She pushed Victory harder, galloping over the

rolling hills, ducking beneath low branches and gritting her teeth against the rough ride. Erik wasn't going to get hurt trying to do her a favor.

She didn't need his help. She'd confront Needleson on her own if she had to.

She crossed onto his land and headed in the general direction of his ranch house and stable. She hoped she wouldn't pass right by it without seeing it through the trees. Her heart pounded with the same rhythm as Victory's hooves upon the turf.

"Mr. Needleson," she called when she spotted the ranch house. "Mr. Needleson!"

Slipping off her horse, she scanned the area but saw no sign of Erik's truck. Had he already been there and gone?

To her relief, John answered her desperate knock almost right away. She looked him over with a critical eye.

He didn't appear to have been in a fight. It was only then that she let out the breath she hadn't even realized she'd been holding.

"What do *you* want?" he demanded, scowling.

He looked like he might slam the door in her face, so she put her hand on the frame to deter him. Her breath came in fast, uneven gasps, and she gulped for air to soothe her stinging lungs.

"I want to know if you set fire to my hay," she said between breaths.

"What?" he roared, opening the door wide.

She cringed. If John *was* the vandal, coming here and accusing him of it to his face probably wasn't the best idea in the world, though it was a little late to figure that out now.

But she hadn't expected to be confronting him on her own. *Where was Erik?*

John looked as if he would spontaneously combust within moments. His face grew increasingly red and creased with angry wrinkles.

"Could I come in?" she suggested, her voice squeaking with tension.

"For what, a cup of coffee?" he retorted.

She shrugged. "I'd rather not talk out here."

"Talk?" He glared at her from under the shelf of his thick gray eyebrows.

She looked away, over his shoulder. "I shouldn't have said what I said. May I come in?"

"It don't matter." He turned and walked back into his ranch-level redbrick house, leaving the door open for her to follow.

Didn't matter that she came in, or didn't matter that she'd accused him of starting that fire, she wondered.

She followed him into the kitchen and watched with increased discomfort as he turned a chair around backward and straddled it, leaning on his forearms.

He didn't gesture for her to sit, so she remained

standing awkwardly in the center of the breakfast nook.

"Why are you here?"

Because I thought Erik would be, she thought. "I've been having some trouble with vandalism at my retreat center," she said aloud.

"That so?"

"Yes. And it's come to my attention that you might have a reason to have carried out those attacks on my property."

"How's that?"

She shook her head. He wasn't giving an inch, neither in word or expression. "I don't know, John. I was hoping you'd tell me."

He snorted. "Not much to tell."

"Then you didn't start that fire?"

He stood up so fast, the chair he was sitting on crashed over underneath him.

Her eyes widened and her breath caught in her throat as she saw the guilty truth in his gaze. "You did start the fire."

He turned toward the window and crossed his arms over his ample chest with a noncommittal grunt.

"Why, John?" she asked quietly, when it was apparent he wasn't going to take out a shotgun. He looked old, tired. Angry and bitter, but not violent. She just didn't sense it in him.

Yet, he'd all but admitted he was responsible for her property damage.

"You don't belong here," he said at last, his voice rough and gravelly.

"So you said. In the notes you left with the bowie knives."

He actually had the grace to cringe. "Yeah, well…"

"I'm no threat to you. Rockhaven won't be any bother. We'll be the best neighbors you've ever had."

He whirled around and caught her gaze. "I don't want neighbors."

She swallowed, but her throat was dry. "I—I had hoped we could be friends," she stammered, then went silent, thinking about his words. Finally she looked up and met his gaze. "What is it you do want? Besides me leaving, I mean," she asked softly.

"Your land."

There it was, out in the open, thought Dixie, not sure whether to be worried or relieved. John turned back toward the window, apparently finished with his part of the conversation.

But Dixie couldn't leave it at that. "If you wanted my land, why didn't you just buy it when it was up for sale? I know several others looked at it before I picked it up."

He leaned his knuckles on the sill. "I did. But I wasn't offering cash."

"Oh." What could she say to that? She could see the tension straining his shoulders, the anger etching deep lines on his face. "I didn't know."

"Don't matter."

"Obviously it does, John, if you feel the need to threaten me."

"Don't matter. You didn't leave." He turned and picked up the chair, resuming his seat, straddling it backward.

"No, I didn't." She cleared her throat and looked away. "And I'm not going to leave. I feel called by God to start this retreat. I hope I can minister to people here."

"Don't bring God into this."

Shaken, she took a mental step backward. Apparently there was more to his anger than just the sale of the land. "I beg your pardon. I didn't mean to offend you."

Leaning on his elbows, he pressed his knuckles against his forehead. "Cathy would have loved your retreat."

Dixie's heart jumped with hope. "She was a Christian?"

"Yeah."

Without thinking, she stood and went to John's side, placing a reassuring hand on his shoulder. "She's in heaven, John."

Tension flared through his shoulders as he bowed his head. But he didn't turn away from her compassion, just quietly accepted it.

"I know," he said at last. He stood and shook her hand from his shoulder.

He took a deep, raspy breath. Dixie was afraid he might cry.

Instead, he darted forward and grabbed her roughly by the shoulders. "That don't change nothing."

Dixie froze at his touch, though his fingers were digging into her skin. He was angry, she sensed, but he wouldn't hurt her.

She met his gaze, willing her own to be calm and reassuring. Was it her imagination, or did the hardness in his eyes soften just a little?

"You're welcome to come visit me at the grand opening this weekend," she said, conscious of how shaky her voice sounded. "I hope you'll come."

His fingers loosened their grip even as his breathing evened out.

He was responding to kindness. There was a good man underneath all that gruff. She just had to reach him.

Relief washed through her.

Thank you, Jesus. Everything would work out in the end.

She was about to tell John so when a deep, angry voice interrupted from the door.

"Get your hands off her, you jerk."

* * *

Dixie yanked herself out of John's grasp and whirled on Erik. "What are you doing here?"

"Looking for you."

"I could say the same," she snapped, frustrated beyond belief. She'd come here to rescue him, and instead had found John Needleson waiting and no sign of Erik anywhere.

And just when she thought she might be making some small progress toward making John a friend, Erik showed up and blew everything sky-high with the first words out of his mouth. Sure, the fire could have been bad, but it wasn't, and Dixie was ready to turn the other cheek. Or at least she had been until Erik burst in on the scene.

It just figured.

Her gaze darted to John, but he'd already closed up. She grieved over the gain she'd once again lost. Two steps backward, even, when Erik strode forward and grabbed John by the collar.

Without a word, he pulled John up until he was eye level, nearly off the floor.

"Just what do you think you're doing?" she demanded, trying to intervene, but neither man appeared to hear her. They were locked in a battle of wills, each refusing to break eye contact.

Dixie sighed loudly and huffed away from them. If there was going to be violence, she wasn't going to be here to see it. "If you *boys* will excuse me, I have work to do."

When Erik heard Dixie make her exit, he slammed John back against the wall and leaned on his forearm to pin the man there. "If I ever see you touch Dixie again…"

He left the threat dangling, not even waiting to see John's reaction. He had a woman to catch.

He stalked out of the house as fast as his boots would let him, but Victory was already gone by the time he got outside.

Fortunately for him, though he wasn't certain she would think so, he'd ridden over on horseback, as well. He had Jazz pointed and trotting in the right direction before he was even mounted.

He urged her forward, desperate to catch up with Dixie. A variety of emotions swirled through his chest. Galloping through the grass, he let himself feel, and examine what he felt.

How could he get angry again so soon after finding peace?

But when he'd gone to tell Dixie of his faith, he'd discovered her missing. And Vic was gone.

He was a cowboy and not a mathematician, but it didn't take him long to put two and two together. He didn't like the answer he came up with.

Dixie had gone to confront John Needleson.

Taking the bull by the horns, just as she always did. He was almost as angry at himself for not realizing earlier what she would do, as he was at her for putting herself in such danger.

They didn't even know yet what the real threat was, though he was certain John Needleson was behind it. And petite Dixie Sullivan had gone to face him down on her own.

Didn't the woman ever think things through? Didn't she realize she could be hurt?

His breath gathered in his throat as he spotted Dixie and Vic through a break in the thick wood. She was trotting slowly as if enjoying the scenery. As if she hadn't a care in the world.

As if he hadn't broken in at the last moment, before John Needleson had harmed her.

He slowed to a trot as he overtook her, grabbing Victory by the bridle.

"What are you doing?" she demanded. "Let go of my horse."

"No."

Dixie tried in vain to pull Victory from his grasp, but he held tight, holding the horse more with the calm words he spoke to the gelding than by the hand gripping his halter.

With a frustrated huff of breath, she threw the reins down and dismounted. "Fine, then, I'll walk."

Erik was off Jazz in record time, pulling both horses' reins over their heads so he could lead them.

"Dixie," he called to her receding figure, but she didn't slow her pace.

"Stubborn woman," he muttered under his breath.

She whirled and marched back in his direction. "I heard that."

He shrugged. Couldn't fault a man for telling the truth.

"Oh, so *I'm* stubborn, now."

So she was getting the hint. Took her long enough. He shrugged again.

"Takes one to know one," she retorted.

He couldn't help it—he had to smile.

"Don't you laugh at me, you big...big... *cowboy*," she exclaimed, making it sound like an insult. When he pulled her toward him, she playfully pounded his chest with her closed fists.

He quickly sobered. "Dixie, you could have been hurt. That's nothing to laugh about."

"I was fine."

"You're always fine, aren't you?" he barked back.

"It's none of your business. *I'm* none of your business," she said as she marched away.

She couldn't have hurt him more if she'd stuck him through with a bull's horn. When would she figure out she *was* his business, not only as her foreman, but because he cared for her?

How did a man who'd never been good with words tell a woman he loved her? That he wanted to spend his life serving God with her right here in the beautiful South Dakota mountains?

That he was scared out of his wits when he thought she might be putting herself in danger?

And who was he to say if she wanted to hear any of it in the first place?

He darted a glance at her. She was still hiking at the same quick pace, unwilling to slow down to speak with him. Her jaw was set and her eyes were flashing.

He'd never been very good at speaking. But maybe speaking wasn't what was required here. What was a man to do with a stubborn woman who wouldn't listen to reason?

He dropped the horses' reins, knowing they wouldn't wander far with all the good meadow grass underneath them, and reached for Dixie before she could grasp a hint of his intentions.

He pulled her toward him and wrapped his arms securely around her waist. "Stubborn woman," he muttered again before sealing her lips with his.

She tensed for a moment, and he was afraid she'd pull away. He knew he'd let her go if she did.

But she surprised him, after that initial shock of contact. She reached up and framed his face with her hands, kissing him back so fiercely he was no longer sure who controlled the moment.

It didn't matter.

He'd gotten his point across, loud and clear. And

he'd better break it off now, before his mind mud-
dled beyond hope.

Whistling for Jazz, he mounted up in one leap and
set off at a full gallop, forcing himself not to look
back, not to dwell on the outcome of his actions.
Who knew if what he'd done would make any difference? She could certainly take it one way or the
other.

And he may, he thought wearily, have just con-
demned himself to a very lonely life.

Dixie brushed her fingers over her lips as she
watched Erik ride away. Victory nudged her side,
looking for a treat. She turned and hugged the horse
around the neck.

"Oh, Victory, what have I done?"

She'd never been kissed like that in her whole
life. Before, Erik's kiss had been sweet and gentle,
unlike today's fierce, passionate outburst.

It frightened her that it was this side of Erik, the
strong, passionate side, she responded to so completely, with her whole heart and soul screaming to
find its missing half. It bordered on the ridiculous
that she had once thought she'd found true love in
Abel Kincaid.

That seemed so very long ago. Now she knew the
truth.

The only man who could ever claim her heart was
Erik.

He made her see life differently, both through her eyes and through her heart. He rescued her even when she didn't need rescuing. The sound of his voice made her toes curl.

She understood what people meant now when they jokingly referred to the "other half" of a married couple. She'd never be whole without Erik in her life. She needed him—to rescue her from her own perfectionist tendencies and stubbornness, and most of all to rescue her from a broken heart.

What a dilemma.

How could she fall in love with a man who didn't know the Lord? It wasn't supposed to happen that way.

And for once in her life, she realized her problem wasn't something she could fix on her own. Part of her wanted to ram the Bible down Erik's throat and force him to believe. Or coax him into it, knowing he'd do anything for her. Hadn't he proven that a thousand times?

But that wasn't how God worked. And in this instance, it was God alone who would have to work.

Dixie's heart wrenched with an almost physical pain. She'd have to wait on God, and she'd never been good at waiting. What if Erik never came around? Would she be able to live knowing she'd see him every day and not be able to share her life with him? But could she leave him behind, and abandon her work in South Dakota?

What was God asking of her?

Giving him one last affectionate rub, she mounted Victory and turned him toward the retreat compound, nudging him with her heel to break into a trot. Feeling the glorious freedom she'd always dreamed of, the wind at her face and the strength of her horse underneath her, she prayed as she'd never prayed in her life.

Chapter Twenty

Erik hadn't planned to kiss her again, and now he wished he hadn't.

Oh, kissing Dixie was all he'd imagined and more. Wonderfully, amazingly so. But the price he paid this time around was just too high.

She hadn't spoken to him since, not for the rest of the week. Not even to give him last-minute instructions on the guests who were arriving in a cluster of cars and vans.

He was uncomfortable with the crowds and the noise, and it took all his willpower not to tuck himself into the stable and stay there until the people were gone.

He could run things around the retreat without being seen by anyone but the staff. But he couldn't see Dixie.

She *mingled*. That was her style.

His was to hang around the shaded corner of the corral until she decided what to do about him.

She would, sooner or later.

She wasn't the type of woman to leave unfinished business. And their kiss definitely fell into that category.

He was still wallowing in the amazing sense of peace God had granted him. He'd lived with hate and bitterness so long, it was hard to imagine living otherwise. Yet now he found he was doing very well without his old, confining emotions.

Now he had room in his heart for Dixie Sullivan, and if there was one thing he learned from their kiss, it was that she felt something for him, as well. God had taken away hate and given him hope.

Patience he had yet to learn.

He leaned against the hitching post, watching Dixie directing traffic. Kids ran back and forth, yelling and chasing each other. He smiled when Dixie captured a preschool girl in her arms and swung her around.

She'd make a great mother, he thought, a lump growing in his throat as he pictured her with children—*their* children. Loving, laughing, teaching.

He swallowed hard.

And she was a great retreat director. Any doubts she had on that score would now have to be erased.

She took the light ribbing about her jeans and hair

with a smile, and happily pointed out the stable where *her* horse was kept.

Surely the church directors could see the obvious—she flourished here. And so would the people she came here to serve.

As the traffic began to slow, a lone horseback rider came down the lane. Had Dixie invited the locals as well as her church family?

She shaded her eyes with her palm and waved at the rider. Erik could see it was a man, but strained to make out his features.

John Needleson.

Dixie obviously didn't know who she was waving to, or she'd be waving him away. And it sure explained why the rider wasn't waving back.

Erik knew he'd been right to stay in her shadow. Didn't this prove it?

Squaring his shoulders, he strode across the driveway to Dixie's side. She wouldn't stand alone on this. He'd send John Needleson packing and be done with it.

Not surprisingly, she ignored him completely. He wished he could say the same about Needleson, but that was not to be.

"John!" she exclaimed as he approached, sounding genuinely thrilled to see him.

Erik whipped his gaze to hers, but she was focused on the approaching rider, her sweet, friendly smile firmly in place.

Needleson tipped his hat politely, though he still kept the gruff frown glued to his face. What was the man doing here, anyway? Had he come to make trouble?

"Miz Sullivan," the older man croaked, then cleared his throat.

"Welcome to Rockhaven," Dixie said, reaching up to shake his hand. "I'm glad you could come."

Erik bristled. She'd *invited* the man who'd nearly destroyed her dream to be a part of this?

Impossible.

John looked at her hand for a moment, then scrubbed his against his jeans and shook her fingers lightly. He looked as uncomfortable as Erik felt.

"Needleson." It wasn't a greeting, and both men knew it. Erik caught John's gaze long enough to warn him.

You mess with Dixie, you mess with me.

John grunted and tipped his head just enough to be a nod. He understood what Erik wasn't saying.

He'd better.

Erik clenched his fists. Anger caught him off guard. The emotion that had once held such a claim on him now felt like a foreign object floating around in his chest. He'd have to tighten the reins on his self-control.

"Join us for dinner," Dixie inserted. "And then we're having a bonfire out here in the square."

John slid from his horse and tipped his hat again. "Yes, ma'am."

"And John—one more thing." She placed a hand on the older man's forearm, and Erik nearly jumped out of his boots. He struggled to exhale, but the same inertia that left him frozen to the spot left the air stagnant in his lungs.

"Yes, ma'am?" John answered in a polite tone.

Too polite, as far as Erik was concerned. He didn't know why he was jealous, except that Dixie had been attracted to an older man in the past. And John was an attractive widower.

"Would you like to see how Victory is faring?"

John nodded. Erik nearly choked. Was she offering to show him her horse in the seclusion of the stable?

"That I would."

At least he looked ashamed, Erik conceded.

Good. He should. And a little salt in his wound wouldn't hurt, for good measure.

"Dixie's a regular horsewoman. You'll have to stay and watch her ride."

John made a strangling noise, and Dixie's face turned the color of a ripe peach.

"I...I'm glad," John said awkwardly, rolling the rim of his hat in his fists.

Dixie turned her flashing eyes on Erik, the first time she'd acknowledged his presence in a week. And she was mad at him again.

The cloud of guilt floated over to him from John. He really wasn't being fair, she chided silently.

He curled the corner of his lip down and frowned. He supposed he wasn't. Dixie hadn't mentioned being a Christian was such hard work. He flashed her an apologetic smile.

She smiled back, and the sun came out in Erik's heart.

"John, I'm sure Erik would accompany you to the barn to help you stable your horse and find Victory."

Erik's heart jumped into his throat. It was his turn to get a message loud and clear. Dixie knew exactly what was going on, even if he hadn't said a word.

Dixie's heart soared. Erik was jealous! She wanted to do a victory dance.

Alone in the kitchen, she pulled some pantry items they'd need for the bonfire. Marshmallows, chocolate bars and graham crackers all went into her stash.

Part of her was annoyed he didn't know how she felt about him, and part of her was elated that he cared. She'd never had a man get jealous over her before. Of course, she hadn't dated much before Abel, and he certainly wasn't the jealous type.

She was glad Erik was.

"I'm going to keep knocking Your door down with prayer, Lord," she whispered aloud. "I've found the completion to the desire of my heart in Erik Wheeler. I'm waiting on You, Lord. Waiting, watching and praying like crazy.''

"Praying for what?''

Dixie whirled around. Erik was leaning against the doorjamb leading outside, his arms crossed over his chest and curiosity written on his face.

"I…er, I was just praying that things would go well,'' she improvised. At least she was telling the truth.

He smiled. "How could it not?''

"I can think of a million reasons,'' she said, shaking her head. "Oh, Erik, I'm so glad you could be here with me tonight.''

Without considering the consequences, she launched herself into his arms. He welcomed her, wrapping her up in the soft feel of flannel and the comforting scent of soap and leather.

"I'm not going anywhere,'' he said in the soft hoarse voice he often used.

She closed her eyes and took a deep, relaxing breath. He stroked her hair soothingly. They stood entwined for several minutes, while she simply let herself relax and listen to the beat of his heart.

But she couldn't stay that way forever. And Erik had questions he wanted her to answer.

"I invited John Needleson,'' she admitted quietly.

He stiffened. "Why?''

"He's a hurting soul, Erik. His wife died.''

"He set fire to your hay. He could have burned down the whole complex."

"He didn't. You said yourself how careful he was that the fire was contained. He wouldn't hurt anyone on purpose."

"Maybe. Fire spreads quickly, Dixie. He couldn't know for sure it wouldn't get worse." He stepped back and looked down at her, his gaze unreadable. When he looked at her like that, she felt the need to justify her actions.

Why should she have to justify anything she chose to do? It was her retreat to do with as she liked.

No.

It was God's retreat, to do with as *He* liked. She allowed her anger to ebb.

"John is angry with God, Erik. You of all people should understand what that feels like."

He flipped his hat off and jammed his fingers in the tangles of his hair. Blowing out a breath, he turned away from her.

"Erik, don't go. I'm sorry. It was wrong of me to bring up your past."

He shook his head. "It's not that."

She reached out to him, grasping him on the shoulder, wanting him to feel what she felt.

"I'm just saying he needs our compassion, not our anger and blame. Forgiveness is a tall order."

"Especially for a man like me?"

"I didn't say that."

"You didn't have to."

Why did he insist on taking her words and twisting them into things she didn't mean? She was hurting him when she meant to be asking for his understanding.

And for his help.

"God has it all under control."

His soft words shocked Dixie like touching an open socket. "What did you say?"

"God's taken care of you this far. Why would He stop now?"

She took a breath and held it, hoping, yet afraid to hope. Needing to ask, but afraid to know.

"How...how do you know? You don't believe in God." Her voice cracked, and she turned back toward the kitchen. "Do you?"

"Dixie." His tentative voice was right behind her, his breath on her neck like a warm hug. "I wanted to tell you earlier this week, but—"

"But I wouldn't talk to you," she interrupted, twirling to meet his gaze. "Does this mean what I think it means?"

He laughed, his steel-blue eyes clear and twinkling.

"I've found out this past week that learning to live the Christian life isn't as easy as learning how to ride a horse. Will you teach me?"

She hugged him tight. "How could I say no, when you've taught me so much?"

He nodded and tugged on the brim of his hat. "Good. Guess I'll be joining you for church this Sunday."

She laughed at the mock-terrified look he gave her and kissed him on the cheek. "They won't eat you. I promise."

"I left John with the horses," he said, coloring red. "Hopefully he won't start any more fires."

She took his big, rough hands in hers and laced their fingers together. "He won't."

"How can you be so sure?" He couldn't help but play devil's advocate, even if he was a new Christian.

"I know. Trust God, Erik."

"Sometimes you have to watch out for yourself, too."

She cuffed him playfully across the rough, dark stubble on his chin. "Is that what you've been doing? Protecting me?"

He snorted. "Trying to."

"I don't know whether to take that as a compliment or a criticism."

His dark blue eyes twinkled with merriment.

What do you think? they challenged playfully.

She shrugged. "I suppose I do need help. Sometimes. But you're kind of an overbearing lug, you know that?"

Grunting like a caveman, he picked her up and threw her over his shoulder fireman-style.

She screeched and pummeled his back with her fists.

"Erik Wheeler, let me go this minute."

"Not until you promise me you'll look out for yourself." He whirled her around in a circle, causing her to scream again as a wave of dizziness assaulted her.

"Erik!" she protested.

"Promise."

"Why should I?" she squeaked.

"Promise."

"I've got you and God to watch out after me."

"Good enough."

She was surprised when he suddenly righted her onto her feet. Clinging to his arm, she waited for her brain to clear.

Or maybe it never would. This funny, fuzzy feeling was kind of nice, now that she thought about it.

She wanted him by her side. Every second from here to eternity. Especially tonight.

"Will you sit with me at the bonfire tonight?" she asked, her heart swelling.

He tipped his hat and winked. "Yep."

Chapter Twenty-One

Erik stared at the flames, wondering how he would get through the night. One arm was right where it belonged—around Dixie's waist. His other hand was tucked in the pocket of his duster, fingering the black velvet box that carried his life's happiness within.

He shot a quick glance at Dixie. A gentle smile playing on her face, she watched the guitar players, singing quietly along with them as they led the group in familiar hymns.

She was a different woman than the one who'd shown up on the land three months ago. And he was a different man.

She wore less makeup, and her hair was worn down around her shoulders instead of in a fancy knot at the back of her neck. Her peaches-and-cream skin had been toughened by the weather, but in Erik's mind, it only added to her attractiveness.

She was beautiful, inside and out. He didn't deserve her.

But he didn't deserve a lot of things. If God could accept him, could he harbor the hope that Dixie would do the same?

He shifted, and she looked up at him, her heart in her eyes. He nearly stopped breathing when the sweet scent of peaches reached his nostrils.

She smiled and reached for his hand.

"Is something wrong?" Dixie thought she glimpsed panic in Erik's eyes before he shadowed them with his hat.

"No. Yes. I…" He looked away.

"Erik." Her heart beat double time as she considered the possibilities. He looked like he wanted to bolt right out of the area.

Was that what he was trying to say? That he didn't want to work for her anymore? Maybe God was leading him in a different direction, just as He had with Abel.

Panic surged through her. She tried to swallow, but couldn't. God wouldn't do that to her again. Not with the way she felt about Erik.

Her gaze darted to where John sat, crumpled up in his sheepskin coat. He wasn't talking to anyone, but he didn't look quite as uncomfortable as he had earlier.

Had he threatened more vandalism, that only Erik knew about?

"Erik, please," she whispered. Not knowing was the worst.

"I...aw Dixie, I..." Again he looked away, his hands stuffed in the pockets of his duster.

But a moment later he turned back, looking as uncomfortable as she'd ever seen him. He stroked a finger down her cheek, then tipped her chin up to meet his earnest gaze.

Then he smiled, that firm, masculine smile that made Dixie's insides dance. Turning her hand palm up, he placed a delicate diamond ring there.

Her eyes glazed with tears. She had prayed. But who would have known?

Who, indeed?

She closed her fingers around the ring, then turned his hand over, palm up, and dropped the ring back in his hands.

Seeing pain cross his features, she held out her left hand and wiggled her ring finger. "Will you marry me?"

She'd never seen such relief on a man's face, nor such joy. Her heart bubbled over with laughter and love.

He swallowed hard, his Adam's apple bobbing with the movement. Silently he placed the ring on her left ring finger, then turned her hand over and kissed the soft spot on her wrist.

Eyes shining, he returned his gaze to hers and said the word they both wanted to hear.

"Yep."

It seemed like hours later, but was probably only minutes, when Erik kissed her cheek and excused himself. Thinking he probably needed to be alone for a little while, she turned her attention back to the bonfire, which, from all appearances, was a success.

Happy faces were everywhere, from the tiniest child to the oldest married couple. These beautiful South Dakota mountains really were a good place to come close to God and feel His presence.

She smiled and held up her hand, admiring how her diamond sparkled in the firelight. Once, she would have wanted a large solitaire, but Erik's choice was so much better for the woman she was now. A small, perfectly cut diamond solitaire surrounded by diamond chips.

That he'd chosen it himself meant so much to her, especially considering that when he'd last been to town, she hadn't been on speaking terms with him.

"Well, folks," the lead guitar player declared. "It seems we have a young fellow here with a very important announcement to make."

Surprised, her head snapped up, and she found herself staring right into Erik's eyes. He'd removed his hat, and was jamming his fingers through his thick hair.

He looked down, then cleared his throat and locked his gaze with Dixie's, determination gleaming in his eyes.

"I just wanted to say, um," he said, then faltered.

Dixie's heart nearly stopped. She felt his keen aversion to speaking in front of people, and it seared in her chest no doubt as much as it did in his.

He just smiled and continued. "I just wanted to say that I'm in love with the sweetest, most beautiful woman in the world. Dixie Sullivan."

There was a collective intake of breath as her dear friends digested the news. Warmth lined her cheeks, but she didn't care a bit. Proudly she stood and took her permanent place by Erik's side.

"And this certified bachelor cowboy has agreed we ought to be a team," she added, linking her arm through his.

Someone started clapping, a lone beat in the darkness.

John Needleson stepped forward into the light of the fire. His brows crunched low over his eyes, but Dixie could see his hands moving in applause.

John smiled and tipped his hat as everyone else joined in the applause for the couple. Erik put his arm around her waist protectively and returned the gesture, tipping his hat to John with his other hand.

Dixie laughed and wrapped her arms around her

cowboy's neck, taking pleasure in being warm, protected, cherished and most of all, loved.

"You didn't have to do that public-speaking thing, you know," she teased, planting small kisses along the rough, strong line of his jaw.

He tipped his head down so their foreheads met and their locked gazes were shadowed from the others. "Yes, I did," he said, his voice low and deep, full of husky emotion. "I botched the proposal, even though I had it all planned out in my head what to say."

She chuckled. "Seems to me it worked out okay."

He smiled with her. "Yep."

"Guess this means you're going to earn your full herd of horses."

He chuckled and pulled her snug into his arms, where she vowed in her heart she would remain for the rest of her life.

"I want everyone to know how much I love you," he continued, his voice scratchy and rough. "You most of all."

Her breath caught in her lungs as he held her close, savoring the words she'd longed to hear.

"I love you, Dixie Sullivan. I don't always say what I feel. But I can't keep this locked inside. I love you. I love you. I love you."

Once he'd said it, it seemed hard to get him to

stop. She chuckled and covered his mouth with her index finger.

"I love you, too, Erik Wheeler." She chuckled again. "And now that you know how to *say* it, why don't you start working on *showing* me just how much you love me."

He grinned and tipped his hat before covering her lips with his own.

"Yep," he whispered over her lips.

And that was all the answer Dixie Sullivan wanted to hear.

* * * * *

Dear Reader,

Writing *Black Hills Bride* brought a couple of "firsts" to my career. You know that old proverb about never saying never?

First, I insisted to my writer friends that I would never write a cowboy hero. Then strong, silent Erik tipped his hat at my muse, and that was the beginning of my cowboy-hero novel!

Also, my books to date have all been crisis-of-faith novels—Christians dealing with their trials and tribulations and growing in Christ through adversity.

Erik was the first fictional character I've brought to a saving faith in Christ through the course of the novel. Rediscovering the awesome grace and mercy of Christ our Savior through Erik's salvation has been a tremendous blessing to me, and I hope for you, as well.

One of my greatest joys is in hearing from my readers. Please write me at P.O. Box 9806, Denver, CO 80209.

In Him,

Deb Kastner

Take 2 inspirational love stories FREE!

PLUS get a FREE surprise gift!

Special Limited-Time Offer

Mail to Steeple Hill Reader Service™

In U.S.	**In Canada**
3010 Walden Ave.	P.O. Box 609
P.O. Box 1867	Fort Erie, Ontario
Buffalo, NY 14240-1867	L2A 5X3

YES! Please send me 2 free Love Inspired® novels and my free surprise gift. Then send me 3 brand-new novels every month, which I will receive months before they appear in bookstores. Bill me at the low price of $3.74 each in the U.S. and $3.96 each in Canada, plus 25¢ delivery and applicable sales tax, if any*. That's the complete price and a saving of over 10% off the cover prices—quite a bargain! I understand that accepting the books and gift places me under no obligation ever to buy any books. I can always return a shipment and cancel at any time. Even if I never buy another book from Steeple Hill, the 2 free books and the surprise gift are mine to keep forever.

303 IEN CM6R
103 IEN CM6Q

Name	(PLEASE PRINT)	
Address	Apt. No.	
City	State/Prov.	Zip/Postal Code

* Terms and prices are subject to change without notice. Sales tax applicable in New York. Canadian residents will be charged applicable provincial taxes and GST. All orders subject to approval. Offer limited to one per household.

INTLI-299

©1998